KV-063-107

KIRKCALDY
DISCARD
J
DISTRICT LIBRARIES

HAMLYN

RUSSIAN FAIRY TALES

RUSSIAN
FAIRY TALES

ILLUSTRATIONS
VLADIMÍR BREHOVSZKÝ

HAMLYN
LONDON / NEW YORK / SYDNEY / TORONTO

KIRKCALDY DISTRICT LIBRARIES

183681

JF/ RUS

CO

RUSSIAN FAIRY TALES

This edition first published 1975 by
The Hamlyn Publishing Group Ltd
Translated by Věra Gissing
Graphic design by Vladimír Janský
Designed and produced by Artia for The Hamlyn Publishing Group Ltd
London ● New York ● Sydney ● Toronto
Astronaut House, Feltham, Middlesex, England
This edition © Artia 1975
Illustrations © Vladimír Brehovszký 1975
ISBN 0 600 37557 9
Printed in Czechoslovakia by Polygrafia
1/01/24/51

INDEX

*My father has three sons. One is called Kuzma, the second Foma and the third —
I can't even remember his name. Actually I am the third son! One day we went after some
ducks. Kuzma took a staff of oak, Foma a staff of maple, and I, the clever one,
a simple staff of wood. We came to the river which was so packed with ducks, we could
hardly see the water! Kuzma swung his stick and threw it at the ducks, but it landed short.
Foma threw his stick too far. I aimed right, but missed the target. We wondered what
to try next. Luckily we came across three boats hidden in the reeds. One was full of holes,
the second leaky and the third completely bottomless. We climbed into the third boat,
caught the ducks and decided to roast one of them. But we had no fire. So my brothers
punched and punched me in the nose, till sparks flew from my eyes — and with these sparks
they lit the fire. We roasted the duck, ate it and settled down to tell each other stories.*

*Kuzma did not know any, however, and Foma had forgotten them all, but I —
the clever one — knew exactly thirty of them.*

Here they are:

CZAR IVAN
AND THE WILD WOLF

In the thirtieth Czardom, which is a mighty kingdom beyond twenty-seven other lands, there once lived a Czar who had two sons. The eldest was called Fjodor and the youngest, Ivan. The Czar was old and frail, and before long he died, leaving his sons to reign after him. Czar Fjodor and Czar Ivan divided the kingdom into two equal parts.

Fjodor decided the time had come for him to marry and started looking for a suitable bride. One day he heard that beyond twenty-seven oceans, in the sixtieth Czardom, there lived a lovely Czarina, so he thought he would go and court her. Brother Ivan went too.

Their golden vessel swiftly glided across the seas, till they reached their destination. There they found the beautiful maiden; but though her beauty was a feast for the eyes, her heart was cold as ice. However, Czar Fjodor wasted no time and married the lovely Czarina in splendid style; then they all turned back, heading for home in their golden vessel.

As it sailed across the seas, they met another ship. Czar Ivan was curious to see who was aboard. He climbed onto the strange ship and found Marja — a maiden so lovely, that the sight of her took his breath away. Never had he realized that anyone on this earth could be so beautiful.

Without hesitation he begged Marja to be his bride, but she replied, "I will not marry until I see my mother and my brother again."

And she refused to tell him who her mother and her brother were.

The unhappy Czar Ivan decided to take his leave and looked to where his own ship should have been—but there was no sign of it on the sea! This was because the sly, wicked Czarina had persuaded Fjodor to sail away, leaving his brother behind, so he alone could rule over all the Czardom. When Ivan realized he was deserted, he grew even more sad. Marja was sorry for him and tried to comfort him.

"Don't worry, Ivan," she said. "Don't complain about your fate. I shall help you."

Spreading a small carpet on the deck, she sat upon it and invited Ivan to do likewise. Then she called out, "Rise, carpet, rise and fly to the skies, above the deep forests, above the high clouds!"

The carpet flew upwards, and in a few moments they arrived in Ivan's own Czardom. As the lovely Marja begged Ivan not to reveal to anyone that she came with him, he hid her out of sight in his room. There they lived together happily. Whenever Czar Ivan left his room, he locked the door behind him, and when he was in it, he bolted the door on the inside.

Some time after, Czar Fjodor and his beautiful, but hard, Czarina returned from the seas to the kingdom, and they were amazed to see Ivan back home. Ivan, however, said not a word about his Marja and her magic carpet. But he had not forgotten how his brother tried to double-cross him.

CZAR IVAN
AND THE WILD WOLF

Time passed. Ivan and his Marja lived together happily, but his brother Fjodor and his wife did nothing but argue and argue. The Czarina was as wicked and as stubborn as she was beautiful. She wanted her way in everything, and not only did she order her poor husband about, she usually ended their quarrels by hitting him.

One day the beautiful, but sly, Czarina said to her husband, "Bring me the boar which ploughs with its snout, levels the soil with its tail and leaves budding corn in its wake. If you don't succeed, I will have you thrown into jail, where you will remain for ever and ever."

Czar Fjodor was terribly frightened, and rushed for help to his brother Ivan.

"Dear Ivan, you've got to help me!" he cried. "After all, you are my brother! My wife has ordered me to fetch her the boar which ploughs with its snout, levels soil with its tail and leaves corn in its wake. If I don't succeed, she will imprison me for ever and ever."

"Now you ask for my help, brother", Czar Ivan answered. "You seem to have forgotten that not long ago you deserted me on a strange ship in the middle of the ocean, so you could take over my half of the kingdom."

Fjodor hung his head in shame. "Please don't be angry with me, brother, for I have regretted leaving you there many times since," he replied. "It was my wife who persuaded me to do so. She is wicked and domineering and I have suffered much in her hands. Don't be angry and please help me!"

Czar Ivan felt sorry for his brother and said, "Very well then. I will give this matter some thought and tell you what is to be done."

With that Ivan departed to his room, where he said to his lovely Marja, "What can I do? My brother begs for my help. His wicked wife has ordered him to bring her the boar which ploughs with its snout, levels with its tail and leaves corn in its wake. Does such a boar exist?"

"Yes, such a boar does exist", Marja replied.

"Can it be caught?" Ivan asked.

"Of course!" was the reply.

"Help me then!" cried Ivan. "I feel so sorry for my brother."

Marja handed a silk scarf to Czar Ivan and said, "When you meet the boar, it will turn on you, intending to tear you to shreds with its fangs. Just wave this scarf before its eyes. Then the wild boar will immediately become as meek as a lamb and will follow you wherever you go."

Czar Ivan strode through the green meadows and open fields. On the first and second days he saw nothing, but during the third day he came across a boar in a field. It was ploughing with its snout, levelling with its tail and leaving budding corn behind it. The moment the boar noticed Ivan, it turned on him, ready to tear him apart. Ivan waved Marja's silk scarf — and straight away the boar became as meek as a lamb and trotted obediently behind him.

Czar Ivan led the boar into the courtyard of the palace. There the animal started

ploughing with its snout, levelling with its tail and leaving corn in its wake. The beautiful, but hard, Czarina saw it all from the window, and ordered the boar to be taken away, before it ruined the whole courtyard. Ivan led the beast out of the palace gates, and with a wave of his scarf released it into the open country.

For some time afterwards Czar Fjodor and his beautiful Czarina lived in peace and happiness. Then the quarrels started once more. One day the Czarina turned to her husband.

"Bring me the mare with forty spots on her hide, with forty colts on each spot and forty mares on each colt!" she ordered. "Otherwise I will have you thrown into the well, where you will remain for ever and ever."

The worried Czar Fjodor went to seek help from his brother.

"This time my wife asks me to bring her the mare with forty spots on her hide, with forty colts on each spot and forty mares on each colt!" he cried. "If I don't succeed, she will have me thrown into the well, where I will remain for ever and ever. Help me, brother Czar, I have no one else to turn to!"

"Wait a minute. I will think this problem over and then I will tell you what is to be done", Ivan replied and retired to his chamber. There he begged the lovely Marja to help to save his brother.

Marja agreed. "Here are some silver reins," she said. "When you come across the mare with the forty spots she will whinny angrily, and charge towards you, intending to trample you to death with her iron hooves. But if you throw the silver reins round her neck, the mare will stop and grow as meek as a lamb. She will follow you wherever you go."

Czar Ivan strode across the wide open fields, through the green pastures. On the first and second days he saw nothing, but during the third day he came across the mare with forty spots on her hide, with forty colts on each spot and forty mares on each colt. The mare turned on him immediately, intending to trample him with her iron hooves. Czar Ivan swiftly threw the silver reins round her neck and the mare grew as tame as a lamb. Then she followed him meekly to the palace.

When Czar Ivan brought into the palace courtyard the mare with forty spots on her hide, with forty colts on each spot and forty mares on each colt, all these colts and all these mares began to neigh loudly, to kick with their iron hooves into doors and gates and to tear the walls down with their sharp fangs. The beautiful Czarina took one look at the damage from her window, and quickly ordered the colts and the mares to be chased out of the grounds, before they completely wrecked the palace. Czar Ivan led the mare with the forty spots from the courtyard, took the silver reins from her neck and released her into the open country.

For some time afterwards Czar Fjodor lived with his beautiful Czarina in peace and happiness once more. But soon the quarrelling began again.

"Bring me the magic sword from the wild wolf. If you don't succeed, I will dress you in a shepherd's cloak and you will tend pigs for ever and ever," was the Czarina's order this time.

(16) 17 CZAR IVAN
     AND THE WILD WOLF

The down-hearted Czar Fjodor came sadly to his brother Ivan, begging for advice.

"Alas, dear brother Ivan, now my wife wants me to bring her the magic sword from the wild wolf," he said. "If I do not succeed, she will turn me into a shepherd and I will have to tend pigs for ever and ever. Please, can you help me?"

"Wait a while," said Czar Ivan. "I will give the matter some thought, then we will see what can be done."

With those words Czar Ivan retired to his chamber and explained to lovely Marja the latest task the beautiful Czarina had given to her husband Fjodor.

"Does such a wild wolf exist?" Ivan asked.

Marja sighed and said sadly, "Yes, it exists."

"And could I take from him the magic sword?" questioned Ivan.

"Perhaps yes, and perhaps no. You could so easily lose your handsome head," said Marja.

"I would rather lose my head, than refuse to help my brother," he exclaimed.

"What are you saying, Czar Ivan." Marja cried. "I would rather lose my head, than have you lose yours. I will help you as much as I can. First you must go to your brother, and ask him to prepare a large ship for a long journey."

Ivan went to his brother Fjodor and told him he would bring the magic sword from the wild wolf, if he prepared a large ship. Czar Fjodor happily agreed and Czar Ivan returned to his room.

The lovely Marja gave him an embroidered towel and a gold ring.

"When you are not able to escape death, wash yourself, wipe yourself with this towel and place this gold ring on your finger," were her instructions.

Then the lovely Marja bade Czar Ivan goodbye, kissing him on his lips. Ivan went down to the harbour in the blue ocean, where he boarded the huge vessel which was specially prepared by Czar Fjodor. Off he sailed towards far distant lands.

He sailed on and on, for a very long time. One year passed, then the second year passed, and finally the very last day of the third year, he arrived at a foreign shore.

Czar Ivan ordered the captain of the ship not to depart before his return. He walked off the ship onto firm land. He strode through open fields, and green pastures, for two days, until, on the third day he came to a green meadow where a white marble castle was built. When Ivan entered, he found an aged, withered woman as white as the moon sitting inside.

"Where are you from and where are you going, young man?" she asked.

"I have been sent from a certain Czardom, a mighty kingdom, to find the wild wolf," Ivan replied.

The old woman grew sad.

"It is lucky you came and unlucky you came," she said. "The wild wolf is my son and he lives here. But your visit will not give you pleasure, only much sorrow. The wild wolf will eat you."

Czar Ivan begged the old lady to help him and to save him from the wild wolf. Eventually she agreed.

"Very well then, I will help you," she said. "I will wrap you up in this length of linen and will start to sew a shirt for the wild wolf from the same cloth. When he comes in, I will not show you to my son, until I see that his heart has softened. Then perhaps he will have pity on you."

The old woman did exactly as she had said. Very soon the wild wolf entered the castle.

"Sniff, sniff, sniff! For three hundred years I have not heard of a human, seen a human, and now suddenly someone has come into my white marble castle. I'll eat him up immediately!" he cried.

"What has got into you, son?" the old woman said. "You have raced all over the place from morning till dusk, so your nostrils are filled with human scent and now you imagine someone is right here."

These words calmed the wild wolf and his heart softened. The old woman took the linen off Ivan.

"Well, well, well! Czar Ivan," the wild wolf remarked. "What brings you here?"

"Fine time to ask, wild wolf!" Czar Ivan replied. "You have given me nothing to drink, nothing to eat and yet you are already asking why I have come."

The old lady hurriedly brought soup and a joint to the table and the wild wolf invited Ivan to sit at the table. Ivan drank a spoonful of soup, while the wild wolf greedily drank the rest; Ivan swallowed one morsel of meat, while the wild wolf gobbled up the rest. The wild wolf had eaten so much he was fit to burst, but poor Ivan was still hungry.

"And now, Czar Ivan, I will eat you," the wolf said. "This is my custom."

"Whyever should you eat me?" Ivan answered.

"Come on, let's have a game of cards. If you're the winner, then eat me up, but if I win, you must not eat me."

The wild wolf took a pack of cards from the table drawer and shuffled them.

"We'll do it differently," he said. "The one who falls asleep first will be the loser."

They sat and played and played. They played for one month; they played for two months. During the third month Czar Ivan started to doze.

"Don't tell me, Czar Ivan, that you are falling asleep?" the wild wolf remarked.

"No, of course not. I was just deep in thought," said Ivan, shaking himself.

"What were you thinking about?"

"I was wondering whether there were more pine woods in the world, or woods with ordinary leaves. I don't know the answer." Ivan replied.

"I can easily find out. I will go and count the woods," said the wild wolf and ran outside. Czar Ivan snuggled down and fell sound asleep.

The wild wolf ran from forest to forest. He ran for one month, for two months and he was still counting. He did not finish counting till the end of the third month, when he

CZAR IVAN
AND THE WILD WOLF

returned to the white marble castle. By then Czar Ivan was well awake and he greeted the wolf merrily.

"Well then, wild wolf, what is the answer?" he asked.

"I have counted up all the woods and found there are fewer pine forests than the others," the wild wolf answered.

They sat at the table again and continued playing cards. They played for one month; they played for two months. During the third month Czar Ivan began to doze again.

"Don't tell me, Czar Ivan, that you are falling asleep," said the wild wolf.

"Of course not, I was just deep in thought," lied Ivan again, shaking himself.

"What were you thinking about?" asked the wild wolf.

"I was wondering whether there were more men or women in the world, but no matter how hard I think, I just cannot find the answer," Ivan replied.

"I can find out easily," said the wild wolf. "I will go and count them."

The wild wolf ran from town to town, from village to village, counting all the time. He counted for one month, for two months, and he didn't finish counting till the end of the third month. Then he returned to the white marble castle. During all this time Czar Ivan slept on and on, only waking just as the wild wolf entered the gate.

"Well then, wild wolf, what is the answer?" he asked, brightly.

"I have counted and counted, and there are certainly more women than men in this world," the wild wolf replied.

Once again they sat at the table and played cards. They played for one month; they played for two months. During the third month Czar Ivan did not just doze; he fell sound asleep.

"Don't tell me, Czar Ivan, that you have fallen asleep," said the wild wolf, but Ivan slept like a log and did not wake. Only when the wolf shook him, did he open his eyes.

"What can I do? I have fallen asleep and lost the wager. But permit me to have a good wash before I die!" he cried.

The wild wolf led Czar Ivan to the well, where he washed himself, dried himself on the embroidered towel given to him by the lovely Marja, then slipped the gold ring on his finger. The wild wolf was surprised.

"Where did you get that towel?" he asked.

"Where should I get it from? It is my towel," replied Ivan.

"How can this be your towel, when it belongs to my own sister?" cried the wild wolf. Then he saw the gold ring and exclaimed, "And this gold ring, why, it is mine!"

Czar Ivan then told him, "The towel and the ring were given to me by my wife, the lovely Marja."

When the wild wolf heard this, he embraced Ivan and kissed him.

"You, Czar Ivan, are the husband of my dear sister, my lovely Marja! Why, you are my brother-in-law!" he cried.

They quickly called to the old lady, the aged, withered woman, as white as the moon and told her that her beautiful daughter Marja was alive and well and married to Ivan. The old lady was so overjoyed, the years seemed to fall from her and she looked much younger. She hastened to prepare a feast to celebrate, bringing varied dishes and wines to the table, and sweets made from honey. During the feast Czar Ivan told them everything, why he had come and how the Czarina was torturing his brother Fjodor.

"Everything will come right in the end," said the wild wolf with a smile, and asked Ivan to sit on his back.

Straight away the wolf rose into the skies, and flew like the wind, like an arrow, over deep forests, under the white clouds. They flew over the blue ocean and saw the ship which had brought Czar Ivan to the shores of the wild wolf's kingdom. They landed on the vessel's deck. Ivan immediately turned to the captain.

"Why did you not wait for me, as I instructed?" he demanded. "Why did you sail onto the wide sea?"

The captain begged forgiveness, explaining that he waited a whole year for Czar Ivan's return. When he failed to come back, he had decided to sail home. Czar Ivan forgave the captain, climbed on the wolf's back, and they flew on.

Soon they were over Ivan's own kingdom and they flew right into his room. As soon as the lovely Marja saw her husband, Czar Ivan, and her dear brother, she wept for joy. While they were talking and smiling and laughing, Ivan suddenly grew quiet and sad. He thought of his brother, Czar Fjodor, who probably at that very moment was tending the swine in the meadow by the forest.

The wild wolf once again told Ivan to jump on his back and together they flew to the forest. They found Czar Fjodor barefooted and dressed in rags, unhappy and hungry. With tears in his eyes he told them how the beautiful, but evil, Czarina had chased him out of the palace and how each day she whipped him with a whip.

The wild wolf was so angry at what he heard that he changed into Czar Fjodor by banging himself against the earth. Then he chased all the swine into the palace. Daringly he entered the chamber of the beautiful Czarina, put her over his knee and whipped her soundly. At first the beautiful Czarina threatened and shouted, then cried, and in the end promised to be good and kind and to turn over a new leaf. And she kept her promise.

The wild wolf turned once more into a beast and then the beautiful Marja spread out her magic carpet. The three of them sat down on it and Marja commanded:

"Rise, carpet, rise, into the skies, fly high over deep forests, over the clouds." With that the carpet rose and took them into the wolf's kingdom.

There the three of them lived on in good health and happiness, eating good meat, drinking good wines, enjoying their days, and sleeping through the nights.

CZAR IVAN
AND THE WILD WOLF

THE COCKEREL
AND THE
MAGIC MILL

Once there was an old man and an old woman who were so poor that when they had nothing left to eat, they went into the forest to gather acorns. After all, acorns are better than no food at all.

When they returned home they began to eat. They did not stop eating until there was only one acorn left on the table. Suddenly it rolled off the table and fell through a hole in the floor.

A few days later a little oak tree started sprouting from the acorn; it grew and grew till it reached the ceiling.

"Make a hole in the ceiling, grandfather, so the oak tree can grow as high as it likes," the old woman said. "At least we will not have to go to the forest for our acorns."

The old man knocked a hole through the ceiling and also through the roof. The oak tree grew and grew till it reached up to Heaven.

Then the old woman said, "Take a sack, grandfather, and climb the tree to gather some acorns, because, once again, we have nothing to eat."

The old man took the sack, climbed the tree, climbing higher and higher, till he reached Heaven itself.

When the old man entered Heaven, he looked round very carefully — and what do you think he saw? A cockerel with a gold comb was sitting there, and next to him stood a little mill. Without further ado the old man snatched the cockerel and the mill, threw them in his sack and slid down to earth.

"Well I never!" the old woman marvelled, when her husband took the cockerel with the gold comb and the little mill out of the sack. "But what shall we eat?"

"I really don't know," answered the old man, idly turning the handle of the mill.

All at once the mill made a strange sound and pancakes and potato cakes flew out of it — so many pancakes and so many potato cakes that the old man and the old woman could not eat them all, even with the cockerel's help.

After that they never went hungry again.

A long time later a baron rode by, and stopped at their cottage.

"Give me something to drink!" he said, "and something to eat, if you have anything."

Grandmother gave the baron a cup of milk and ground him some pancakes and potato cakes with the magic mill.

"Well I never," marvelled the baron. "Sell me the magic mill, old woman!"

"No I won't," she answered, shaking her head.

"If you won't sell, I'll just take it," the baron laughed slyly. He grabbed the mill and rode off.

(22) 23   THE COCKEREL
             AND THE MAGIC MILL

The old man and the old woman raved, complained, sobbed and cried, but that did not bring back their mill.

Then the cockerel with the gold comb said, "Stop crying and complaining! I will bring the mill back."

And he flew after the baron.

When he reached the courtyard, he perched on the gates and started to shout.

"Thieving baron, thieving baron! Give me back the magic mill!" he crowed.

The baron heard him and said to his servant, "Drown that cockerel in the well!"

The servant caught the cockerel, and threw him into the well.

But the cockerel said, "Beak, beak, spill all that water."

When the cockerel had drank all the water, he flew out of the well, perched on the window-sill and crowed even louder.

"Thieving baron, thieving baron, give me back the magic mill!"

The baron was furious. "You confounded cockerel!" he shouted. "I'll have the cook throw you in the oven!"

The cook caught the cockerel, and threw him into the red hot oven.

But the cockerel said, "Beak, beak, drink up all the water."

And the water from the well cooled the boiling oven.

The cockerel flew out of it, straight into the baron's rooms. Then he cried at the top of his voice, "Thieving baron, thieving baron, give me back the magic mill!"

The baron was surrounded by many visitors, and he was just showing them the magic mill. When all the people heard the cockerel's noise, they grew frightened and scampered to their homes. The baron ran after them and the cockerel with the gold comb swiftly snatched the magic mill and hastened back to the old man and the old woman. They were very thrilled to have the cockerel and the magic mill back again, and they never went hungry again. The mill kept on grinding pancakes and potato cakes, and more potato cakes and pancakes. That is all I know, so I can't tell you any more.

IVAN BYKOVICH /IVAN BULL/

Somewhere beyond the red sea, beyond the blue forest, beyond the glass mountain, and beyond the straw town where they sift water and pour sand, stood a mighty Czardom. The Czar and the Czarina ruled well, but they were most unhappy because they had no children.

One day, when the Czarina strolled through the royal gardens, she suddenly met a grey old woman who said to her, "I know why you are so unhappy, your royal highness! But I know how to chase away your sadness! Order your servant to catch the trout with the silver fin from the lake, then have soup made with the fish. When you have drunk this soup, you will have a son."

As soon as the old woman had spoken, she disappeared as mysteriously as she had appeared.

The Czarina ordered fishermen to catch the trout with the silver fin in the lake. Then her maid cooked the fish soup. The Czarina drank most of it, the maid finished the rest and took the slops to the bull in the sty. Some time afterwards the Czarina gave birth to little Ivan Czar; the maid gave birth to Ivan Maiden and the bull — to Ivan Bull.

The three boys grew and grew so rapidly, that at the end of twelve months they were as tall and as strong as others in their teens.

Then the three Ivans decided to roam the fields, and indeed to roam the wide world, so they would see other regions.

They entered the stables to choose their horses.

Ivan Czar and Ivan Maiden chose handsome, brave mares, but Ivan Bull was not so lucky. The moment he patted the back of any horse, it fell to the ground. Then he went into the deep cellar and there he found a horse the colour of the night; sparks flew from its eyes and steam puffed from its nostrils. When Ivan Bull patted this horse on its back, it did not fall down.

"This one is for me," Ivan Bull said to himself and led the horse outside.

The three Ivans galloped over the fields; they rode on and on, till they reached the river Smorodina, at the spot where a stone bridge spanned it.

"Let us put up our tent here and stay overnight," said Ivan Bull.

They pitched their tent right by the bridge and drew lots to see which one of them would stand guard that night. It happened to be Ivan Czar.

Ivan Maiden and Ivan Bull curled up in the tent, while Ivan Czar stood on guard by the stone bridge. Ivan Bull just could not fall asleep. He turned and tossed on the ground, till he gave up.

"I'll have a look to see how Ivan Czar is guarding us," he thought.

Ivan Bull strolled to the stone bridge and found Ivan Czar slumped on the shore, snoring so loudly the whole bridge was shaking.

Ivan Bull shook his head in disgust and then noticed that a terrible looking dragon with three heads was riding towards him along the bridge. His horse nervously stumbled.

"Why do you stumble, my mare?" asked the dragon.

The magnificent mare replied, "I stumble and stumble because I am terrified."

The dragon roared with laughter. "What can you be afraid of?" he asked. "There is only one creature on earth we have to fear, and that is Ivan Bull."

"That's me!" cried Ivan Bull. And with one swift sweep of his sword he cut off the dragon's three heads. He threw the heads and the body into the river Smorodina, but let his horse gallop away into the pasture. Then he went to sleep.

In the morning Ivan Bull asked Ivan Czar, "How did you get on, being on guard?"

"Very well, very well," Ivan Czar nodded his head eagerly. "Everything was so quiet all night, not a single leaf moved."

The three of them then rode out into the wide open country. They rode and rode, but in the evening returned again to the stone bridge and their tent. It was Ivan Maiden's turn to stand guard.

Once again Ivan Bull could not go to sleep; he tossed and turned and in the end went to see how well Ivan Maiden was guarding them. He found him slumped on the shore, sleeping and snoring so loudly, that the stone bridge was shaking.

Ivan Bull shook his head in disgust and then noticed a six-headed, terrible looking dragon riding towards him along the bridge. His horse was stumbling nervously.

The dreadful dragon cried, "Why do you stumble, my mare? Surely you are not afraid! There is only one creature on this earth we must fear, and that is Ivan Bull!"

"That's me!" cried Ivan Bull, brandishing his sword. With one swipe he cut off three heads, and with the second swipe he cut off the other three. He threw the dragon's body and all his heads into the river Smorodina, sent his horse into the open country and then went to sleep.

In the morning Ivan Bull asked Ivan Maiden, "How did you enjoy being on guard, brother?"

"Very much, very much," Ivan Maiden answered smugly. "Everything was silent and still all night; not even a blade of grass moved."

The three of them then rode out into the vast fields. They rode on and on, but in the evening returned once again to the stone bridge.

This time it was Ivan Bull's turn to stand guard. Before he left, he turned to his brothers.

"Tonight I will stand guard, but you, brothers, must also stay awake!" he said. "When my horse begins to stamp, let him loose!"

Ivan Bull went to the stone bridge and waited. After some time he saw a horrific nine-headed dragon riding along the bridge towards him. The dragon was merry, but his horse stumbled nervously.

"Why do you stumble, my mare? Surely you are not afraid!"

The horse answered, "I am afraid, very much afraid, afraid of Ivan Bull."

The dragon roared with laughter. "You don't have to fear Ivan Bull," he said. "I'll sit him on the palm of my hand, and with the other hand squash him like a fly."

"We shall see!" cried Ivan Bull.

Brandishing his sword, he swung it for the first time and sliced off three heads; he swung it for the second time and cut off three more heads; but before he had a chance to take the third swipe, the horrific nine-headed dragon glued the fallen heads back again with its fiery finger, and it was as before with all the nine heads.

They fought on and on, but as quickly as Ivan Bull sliced off the dragon's heads, the dragon glued them back with its fiery finger, before all nine were cut off. Ivan Bull realized that he could not beat the nine-headed dragon with its fiery finger.

Just then his horse began to stamp its feet wildly. It made such a noise with its hooves, that the stone bridge started to shake, and the water from the river Smorodina started to spill on to the shore.

But Ivan Czar and Ivan Maiden were so soundly asleep they did not hear the stamping, and did not let the horse go.

The dragon was now furiously attacking Ivan Bull, pinning him to the ground. Ivan Bull only just managed to slip off his boot, throw it into the white tent and break in two the reins of his horse. Quick as lightning the horse began to attack the dragon.

While it trampled on the dragon with its hooves, Ivan Bull swiftly cut off the monster's fiery finger, and after that it was easy to slice off all the heads. When all was done, Ivan retired to his tent and fell asleep.

The next morning he said to his brothers, "Why didn't you release my horse, when he stamped his feet during the night?"

The brothers seemed surprised.

"We did not hear a thing," they said. "It was so quiet, not a single leaf rustled, not a blade of grass moved in the breeze."

Ivan Bull led Ivan Czar and Ivan Maiden to the stone bridge, and, pointing to the dragons' eighteen heads and the three trunks in the river Smorodina, he told them everything that happened.

Afterwards they journeyed on and on, till they arrived by a large, wooden house, knocked together carelessly from unpolished planks of oak. There were neither windows, nor doors, and a rough rock took the place of the roof.

"You go on ahead, brothers," said Ivan Bull, "I'll have a look round."

The other two Ivans rode on, while Ivan Bull climbed the rough rock, peered inside and saw the three wives of the three horrific dragons complaining to an old hag.

The first was saying, "Alas, mother, that confounded Ivan Bull killed my husband — your son — the three-headed dragon.

The old hag replied, "You can't bring him back to life, but you can avenge him!

In a wide open field turn yourself into a feather-bed. Ivan Bull will lie on it and will burn to ashes."

The second wife said, "Alas, mother, that confounded Ivan Bull killed your son — my husband—the six-headed dragon."

The old hag once again replied, "You can't bring him back to life, but you can avenge him! Turn yourself into a well with a gold goblet. Ivan Bull will have a drink and will burn to ashes."

The third wife complained, "Alas, mother, that confounded Ivan Bull killed your son — my husband — the nine-headed dragon."

The old hag replied, "You too cannot bring him back to life, but you must avenge him. In a wide open field, turn yourself into an apple tree with red apples. When Ivan Bull picks one, he will burn to ashes. And even if all this fails, then I will avenge the death of my three sons."

When Ivan Bull had listened to all this, he jumped astride his horse and caught up with his brothers.

The three Ivans rode on and on, and as they were tiring, they wanted to go to sleep. Suddenly they saw a large field with a lovely soft feather-bed in it.

"Let us rest!" Ivan Czar and Ivan Maiden shouted together.

Ivan Bull, however, took off his glove, tossed it on to the bed, and immediately it burned to ashes. Then he chopped up the bed with his sword and on they rode.

They rode on and on, until they became parched with thirst. All of a sudden a well stood before them, a golden goblet by its side.

"Let's have a drink!" cried Ivan Czar and Ivan Maiden.

But Ivan Bull took his other glove off, tossed it into the well, and the glove burned to ashes. He then chopped up the well with his sharp sword and on they rode.

They rode on and on, till they were very hungry. To their surprise they saw an apple tree laden with red apples in the middle of a field.

"Let's eat!" cried Ivan Czar and Ivan Maiden.

Ivan Bull, however, took off his cap, threw it into the tree branches, and the cap burned to ashes. Then he chopped up the apple tree with his sharp sword and on they rode.

Suddenly they realized someone was flying behind them.

It was the old hag, the mother of the dragons, flying in a huge bowl, propelling herself with a mallet. She was catching up with the brothers.

Then they saw a forge and the blacksmith Kuzma at work. He welcomed the brothers and closed the iron door behind them, and the old hag screeched to a halt outside.

"Open the door, blacksmith Kuzma!" the old hag screamed, banging on the door. "I will gulp down Ivan Bull, as if he were a raspberry."

"I will let you have Ivan Bull only when you have licked right through the iron door with your tongue!" blacksmith Kuzma shouted back.

The old hag licked the iron door; she licked and licked and licked and licked till her tongue came right through into the forge. That was what Ivan Bull was waiting for. He ran out and with one blow of his sword severed the old hag's head.

This is how Ivan Bull and his brothers got rid of the three horrific dragons and their mother—the old hag.

LAZYBONES NODDY

Now listen carefully and keep quiet, otherwise who knows what might happen! The stove could fall on top of you, so could the ceiling, and you would have to leap out of the window and run far away — if you were still in one piece! So pay attention!

In a certain village there once lived three brothers; the youngest was called Lazybones Noddy. The older two worked hard as merchants, but all Noddy ever did was to sleep above the stove.

One day the elder brothers were leaving for the town and they said to Noddy, "We shall be away a week. Obey our wives, help them, and if you behave we will bring you back some gingerbread and vodka."

"Very well," agreed Noddy. Then he turned on his side and went back to sleep as his brothers rode off.

The next day their wives turned to Noddy and said, "Noddy, climb off that stove and fetch us some water!" But Noddy snored on, hearing nothing.

"Noddy, remember your promise?" the wives insisted. "If you don't fetch the water, you won't get the gingerbread, or vodka, when our husbands return."

Noddy sighed, slithered off the stove, took the pail and went to the river. Chopping a hole in the ice, he filled the pail with water, then noticed he had caught a pike in it.

"We'll have you fried," he said, licking his lips.

To his surprise, the pike pleaded with Noddy in a human voice, "Let me go, Noddy. Put me back into the river. If you let me go, I will fulfil your every wish."

Noddy looked startled, but the pike continued, "All you have to do, is to say: 'With the command of the pike, this wish I would like' and every wish will be fulfilled."

Noddy shrugged his shoulders, put the pike back into the river and said, "With the command of the pike, this wish I would like: let the pail run home on its own, without a single drop of water being spilled."

As soon as this was said, the pail raced home and Noddy sauntered behind it, as if he were going for a stroll.

The wives were very surprised to see the pail run in on its own, but they could not make head nor tail of Noddy's explanation. No wonder, too, for he was not only lazy, but also very silly.

The next day the wives turned to Noddy, "Noddy, get off that stove and chop some wood."

But Noddy snored on and heard nothing. The wives were getting annoyed. "Remember your promise, Noddy. If you don't chop the wood, you won't get the gingerbread, or vodka, when our husbands return."

This woke Noddy up, but all he did was to whisper, "With the command of the pike, this wish I would like: let the hatchet chop a tidy pile of fire-wood."

The hatchet obediently started to chop the wood and leave the logs in a neat pile. The wives were even more surprised, but they still could not get any sense out of Noddy.

The third day they turned to him and said, "Get off that stove, Noddy, and go into the wood to fetch some logs. If you don't go, you won't get the gingerbread, or vodka, when our husbands return from town."

Noddy sighed, slithered off the stove and climbed upon the sledge, but he did not bother to strap a horse to it, or to take a hatchet and a saw. The wives gaped at him, but Noddy just said with a wave of his hand, "Why race the horses, and why bother with a saw and a hatchet?" Then he added, "With the command of the pike, this wish I would like: let the sledge race to the wood, let it get the logs, pile them on, return back home and leave them tidily in the yard."

No sooner said, than done! The sledge raced towards the woods all on its own, with Noddy sitting calmly on it. People began to assemble from all sides, for none of them had ever seen such a sight. They hopped around, shouting, "Look at silly Noddy! He is riding on a sledge, without being pulled by a horse, or pushed by a bull."

Noddy took no notice of them whatever and the sledge pushed several of them into a snowdrift, and knocked some of them into the river. Soon he reached the forest. In a twinkling of an eye the sledge was fully laden, and he was off back home.

The people were still shouting, "Look at that silly Noddy! He rides like a lord, knocking us over, pushing us into the snowdrifts, or the river."

Noddy took no notice, and once more knocked some into the river, others into the snowdrifts. Soon he was back home. The logs stacked themselves in a neat pile in the yard and Noddy was nodding off again in his favourite place above the hot stove.

The wives now left Noddy alone. The folk from the village were so cross with him, and they were afraid of what he might do next. As it happened, the Czar himself heard the story and ordered his captain to bring Noddy to him.

The captain came to Noddy and said, "Noddy, climb off that stove, for you are to go to his Majesty, the Czar."

But Noddy did not feel like it so he turned on his other side and snored on.

"Didn't you hear?" The captain grew very angry and started to pull Noddy off the stove.

Noddy simply grunted, "With the command of the pike, this wish I would like: let this captain get a really sound beating."

The poker jumped out from the side of the stove and gave the captain the beating of his life. His head cast down in shame and his backside all sore, he returned to the Czar, complaining bitterly about how badly he had fared with silly Noddy.

Then the Czar sent his general after Noddy.

The general was more clever. He went to the wives first and asked them what Noddy liked best and then began to wake him up.

"Get up, Noddy, his Majesty the Czar wants you to visit him. He has prepared a feast of gingerbread and vodka," he said.

"Gingerbread and vodka!" marvelled Noddy, licking his lips. "Very well then, you go on ahead, and I'll catch you up."

The general went back to the Czar, but Noddy had another little nap. Then he said, "With the command of the pike, this wish I would like: let the stove take me to the Czar."

No sooner had he spoken, than the oven drove off, knocking down half the cottage wall. It roared down the road all the way to Petersburg.

What a commotion they caused when they arrived in the Czar's palace! The Czar had such a shock that he fell off his throne, and his daughter laughed so much that she doubled up with mirth. The general just shrugged his shoulders and said calmly, "I have done exactly what you commanded, your Majesty, the Czar. Silly Noddy is here, and so is his stove."

The Czar quickly recovered, and turning to Noddy, shouted:

"What pranks you keep on getting up to in my Czardom. You drive like the devil, knocking people down, into rivers, into snowdrifts."

"They should keep out of my way," Noddy grumbled, and looked at the Czar's daughter. She was really beautiful and Noddy fell in love with her at first sight. So he whispered quickly, "With the command of the pike, this wish I would like: let the Czar's daughter fall in love with me."

In the meantime the Czar raved and ranted, until the hills shook. Noddy did not like it at all, so he said, "With the command of the pike, this wish I would like: let the stove take me back home."

Straight away the stove started on its homeward journey. The Czar was dumbfounded and the young Czarina just wailed and sobbed, saying she could not live even a moment without silly Noddy and that she must marry him. But Noddy was already back home, snoring away loudly over the stove.

Now nobody knew what to do about Noddy. The village folk complained about him, the brothers' wives were afraid of him, the Czar thought in vain how he could get the better of him, and his daughter cried for him all day long.

The general, however, smiled slyly. He knew how to trap Noddy. He bought a basket full of gingerbread and bottles of vodka, and rode to his cottage with a troop of his soldiers. He sat by him on the stove, fed him with gingerbread and vodka and very soon Noddy was so full and bloated, he fell asleep. The soldiers picked him up immediately, put him into a waiting carriage and sped back to the Czar's palace. Noddy slept on and on.

"Got you at last!" the Czar cried joyfully, when he saw the sleeping Noddy in the carriage.

He ordered the soldiers to put Noddy inside a dark barrel, and to put the young Czarina with him too, as she did not want to be parted from him for a single moment. Then the barrel was thrown into the sea and was swept away by the current.

Noddy awoke three days later and wondered where on earth he was.

"We are shut in a barrel," wailed the Czarina. "Goodness knows where we are."

"Hm," remarked Noddy, scratching his head. Then he remembered the pike and said, "With the command of the pike, this wish I would like: let the waves toss us onto some shore."

The moment he had spoken, they were on the shore. They climbed out of the barrel, but saw that they had landed on a desolate island; there was not a person, nor a single building to be seen.

"We have jumped out of the frying pan into the fire," cried the Czarina. "Here we will die with hunger and cold! We might as well have drowned in the sea."

Noddy only smiled and said, "With the command of the pike, this wish I would like: build a magnificent palace fit for a Czar, with gold spires and one thousand servants."

Lo and behold, straight away a magnificent palace was before them, and the servants welcomed Noddy and the Czarina and led them inside.

It was a truly beautiful palace, with gold, silver and marble everywhere, and deep, lush carpets on the floors. But Noddy was most withdrawn and quiet, he fidgeted and fidgeted until the Czarina asked, "What is the matter with you, Noddy? Is there something here you don't like?"

"I like it all, I don't like it all," muttered Noddy. "But I miss my old stove."

"What on earth do you want your old stove for?" laughed the Czarina. "We have soft beds with feather covers; they are much better than your old stove."

"No they're not." Noddy shook his head sadly. "A stove is a stove. Nothing is quite like it."

"Then bring it here, with your magic," advised the Czarina.

"I can't really do that," Noddy answered. "Now that I am the Czar's son-in-law, I shall have to learn to manage without the stove. It just doesn't go with a Czar's palace."

From that day on Noddy and his Czarina lived on royally in their gold palace, and news of the palace on the desolate island started to spread all over the region until it came at last to the ears of the Czar himself.

"Well now!" said the Czar angrily. "What cheeky person has dared to build a palace on my island, without even asking permission first? I am, after all, the Czar, and not just a nobody."

He gave the order to have his golden ship prepared to sail, and off he went towards the island. When the Czar stepped ashore, he was immediately welcomed by Noddy's Mayor, and taken to the best chamber of the palace, where he was welcomed by Noddy and his bride.

At first the Czar did not even recognize Noddy — for he had never seen him so beautifully dressed — but he recognized his daughter straight away and was so amazed, that he could not speak. When he recovered, he said, "So this is where you have settled. How grand it is!"

"Yes, father," said the Czarina meekly and embraced the Czar. "I do hope you're not annoyed with us."

"Maybe I am, and maybe I'm not. What would be the point of it?" sighed the Czar. "I think it would be best for you both to move into my palace with me, and leave this one just for the summer vacation, when Noddy may want to do some fishing."

So it all ended happily. Noddy and his Czarina went to live in the Czar's palace. They lived on and on, enjoying life, good times, good food, sweet wines and vodka.

THE RUNAWAY SOLDIER
AND PETER THE CZAR

Long ago, when Czar Peter the Great ruled Russia, there lived a farmer, who had two sons. The eldest son joined the army. They shaved his head, dressed him in an army coat, gave him a sword and a gun and told him to serve his country. The new recruit served well and became a good soldier. He was lucky too, and in a matter of two years, he was promoted to the rank of general.

Just at that time it was the turn of the farmer's youngest son to go into the army, and it happened that he was placed in the very regiment where his brother was a general. The youngest son was delighted to recognize his own brother in a general's uniform. He thought how nice it would be to serve under him. How wrong he was! The general was ashamed of his brother and wanted nothing to do with him. He turned on him nastily, "I don't want to know you. Don't come near me!"

The young soldier was put on guard at the general's house where a great ball was being held. Many officers, noblemen, beautiful women and important people gathered, and they were all merry; feasting, drinking, laughing and dancing. The young soldier was so sad to see his brother enjoying himself and yet not sparing him a single thought, that he started to cry bitterly. One of the lovely ladies who was passing asked:

"Why are you crying, soldier?"

"Because my brother the general is dancing and enjoying himself and does not care about me at all."

The lovely lady went to the general and told him what she had heard. The general was furious; he denied everything and ordered his brother to be taken away from his post and to be given three hundred lashes the next morning. The young soldier was so upset that he ran away from his regiment that very night.

He walked on and on, not caring where he went, until he came to a deep forest. He decided to live there, for it seemed better to live on wild berries and roots, than to put up with such injustice from his own brother.

At that particular time Czar Peter the Great rode into the very same forest with his huntsmen. On the edge of the forest a handsome stag sprang out of the bracken and the Czar went in its pursuit. The stag leapt over bushes and rocks and the Czar kept on its heels, but in the end the stag escaped him. The Czar then stopped and looked around. All round him were only trees and dense thicket; there was not a path to be seen and his huntsmen were goodness knows where! He realized he was completely lost. For the rest of the day he tried to find his way out, unsuccessfully. Suddenly he heard someone singing nearby. He followed the sound of the voice, and saw the runaway soldier sitting on a boulder.

"Good day, soldier!"

"Good day to you, too. Where have you appeared from?"

"I am one of the Czar's servants, and I have lost my way during the hunt. Please, show me the path out of this forest."

"I will lead you out, but not today. Already it is dark and you would not reach the town. You will have to spend the night in the forest."

The Czar was not exactly keen on the idea, but there was nothing else he could do.

"If only I had a roof over my head," he sighed.

"In that case, let us both take a look around," said the soldier. "There may be a cottage somewhere nearby."

Climbing to the top of a tree, he gazed round and saw a flickering light not far away.

"Shall we try it?" he said. "We may be able to spend the night there."

As they walked, the Czar started to question the soldier, "Which regiment are you from?"

"I do not belong to any regiment, my friend. I am a deserter."

"Oh, I see. And why did you run away?"

The soldier told him truthfully how his own brother had wronged him.

Soon they came to a tiny cottage. They tethered their horses and went inside. An ugly old woman sat by the stove and frowned at them angrily.

"Can you give us something to eat, grandmother?" asked the soldier. "We can sleep in the hay in your loft."

"I have nothing to eat," the old hag grumbled.

"I don't think that it is so," said the soldier. "I can smell meat roasting."

He walked over to the stove and took a roast lamb from the oven. In the pantry he found enough food for a whole regiment, and in the cellar many bottles of wine. They ate and they drank and then climbed into the loft to sleep.

"There is something very peculiar about this place," remarked the soldier, "I think we had better take turns to stand guard."

It was the Czar's turn first. The soldier lent him his sword, but the Czar found it difficult to keep awake. His eyes kept closing.

"Surely you're not sleeping?" called the soldier.

"No, of course not, I am just deep in thought."

Then the Czar fell into a really deep sleep. He tumbled on the floor and snored loudly.

"I should like to see you in my regiment," sighed the soldier, and, taking the sword, kept guard himself.

A little while later he heard voices below, and laughter and shouting. The robbers who lived in the cottage had returned home.

"Any news, old woman?" they were shouting.

"We have two visitors. They have eaten the supper and now they are sleeping in the loft."

"I'll take a look at those visitors," said one of the robbers. Picking up a sharp knife,

THE RUNAWAY SOLDIER
        AND PETER THE CZAR

he climbed the stairs to the loft, intending to kill them. But the moment his head appeared, the soldier swung his sword and cut it right off. Then he dragged the body up into the loft.

The other robbers waited for their friend to return. When he failed to do so, another one went up to see what had happened. The soldier gave him exactly the same treatment as the first robber. And the rest of them met the same fate. The leader of the robbers was the last one to come up, and he too finished up without his head. After this the soldier flopped down into the hay, and slept soundly.

When the Czar woke up in the morning, he was horrified to see blood, several heads and headless corpses all round him. He shook the soldier from his sleep, "What on earth have you been doing during the night?"

The soldier told him all that had happened and scolded the Czar for being such a bad guard, and falling asleep. Then they went downstairs and the soldier shouted at the old hag,

"So you, wicked woman, are the robbers' accomplice! Show me where you have hidden their loot!"

The old hag was shaking with fear and her teeth were chattering so much that she could not speak, but she pulled forward a chest and unlocked it.

It was filled to the brim with gold coins.

The soldier pushed as many as he could into his pockets and said to the Czar, "Take some, too!"

"I don't need any," he replied. "The Czar is very rich and he pays me well. Take my share too."

So the soldier filled his army bag with the gold coins. They left the cottage, and some time later came to the edge of the forest where a road led to the town. There they bade each other goodbye. The Czar said to the soldier:

"Many thanks for everything, my friend. Please come and visit me in the palace. Just ask for Peter; everyone knows me."

"I don't think I should come. Remember I am a deserter and they would lock me up."

"Don't worry about that! The Czar likes me and I am sure I can persuade him to spare you. You must come tomorrow."

"Very well then," the soldier agreed, and they went their separate ways.

As soon as the Czar returned to the palace, he told all his guardsmen, servants and patrols that he was expecting a certain soldier the following day and that they should treat him like a general.

When the soldier arrived at the palace, all the guards at the gates stood to attention as if he were a general.

The soldier was surprised. "Who are you saluting?"

"You, sir."

The soldier took a handful of coins from his pockets, gave them to the guardsmen and walked on. The same thing happened by the next gate, and the next. The soldier had given away so many gold coins, he was getting annoyed, "That servant of the Czar is a real gossip. He must have told everyone how much money I have, and now they are all trying to get round me."

He reached the main courtyard, and stood astounded. It was filled with soldiers, officers, even his brother the general was there; and in front of them was the Czar himself.

"Oh dear, what have I done," muttered the soldier worriedly, when he recognized the Czar to be yesterday's friend. "How will all this end?"

In fact it ended very well. The Czar welcomed him as an old friend and told everyone what a brave soldier he was and how he had saved his life. Then he added, "As you are such a hero, I promote you to the rank of general."

The drums beat loudly and the band played merrily and everyone present shouted hurrah! They were all happy — that is all but the soldier's elder brother. The Czar had demoted him to the rank of an ordinary soldier. It was his punishment for not wanting to acknowledge his own brother.

Czar Peter was indeed a very just man.

THE GREEDY FOX
AND KUZMA GETRICH

Once upon a time, in a woodland meadow, there lived a young man called Kuzma Getrich. All he had in the world was a battered pair of trousers and five hens, nothing else.

One day Kuzma went to hunt in the wood. While he was out, a greedy fox ran into his cottage, killed one of the hens, roasted it and ate it, and then ran away.

When Kuzma returned, he counted the hens. One was missing; only four were left. "The wolf must have taken it," he sighed.

The next day he was off hunting again. On the way he met the fox.

"Where are you going, Kuzma?" it asked.

"To hunt in the forest!"

"I wish you luck," cried the fox slyly and raced to the cottage.

It killed the second hen, roasted and ate it, then ran off.

When Kuzma returned, he counted the hens. Again one was missing. There were only three left.

"I bet it wasn't the wolf, but that sly fox!"

The next day, before he left for the forest, Kuzma closed all the windows firmly and locked the door. Again he met the fox.

"Where are you going, Kuzma?"

"To hunt in the forest!"

"The best of luck," cried the fox, and raced towards the cottage.

But the cottage was locked and all windows firmly closed. The fox ran round the cottage, trying in vain to get in. Eventually it climbed onto the roof and slithered down the chimney. By the time it crawled into the kitchen, Kuzma was back again.

"What a fine thief you are! Just you wait, you won't get out of this alive!"

"Leave me alone, Kuzma," cried the fox. "Why don't you roast me another hen. I will help you to turn your luck."

Kuzma roasted the hen, the fox gobbled it up, ran out into the clearing and lay down to rest. Just then the wolf ran past.

"Why are you sprawled here, fox?"

"You would be sprawled here too, if you had been with me at the Czar's palace for lunch. I ate so much I thought my tummy would burst; and I am going back tomorrow."

"Listen, fox, can I come with you?" the wolf asked.

"Why not? The Czar has so much food; everything you could want. Why don't you bring with you forty times forty wolves, then our visit will be worth while."

The wolf gathered together forty times forty wolves and the next morning they all ran to the Czar's palace with the fox. The fox left all the wolves in the courtyard and went

THE GREEDY FOX
AND KUZMA GETRICH

to the Czar, "Mighty Czar, I have come to you with a gift from my master Kuzma Getrich. He sends you forty times forty wolves."

The Czar thanked the fox, ordered the wolves to be caught and skinned, and said to himself, "That Kuzma Getrich must be a rich man."

The fox returned to Kuzma and said, "Please roast me yet another hen. I promise to turn your luck for the better."

Kuzma roasted the bird, the fox gobbled it up and ran out into the clearing to rest. A bear passed by.

"Why are you lounging here, fox?"

"You wouldn't be able to move either, if you had been with me at the Czar's palace for lunch. I ate so much I thought my tummy would burst; and I am going again tomorrow."

The bear asked, "Listen, fox, can I come with you tomorrow?"

"Why not? The Czar has so much food and drink, there is everything you could want. Bring with you another forty times forty bears."

The bear found forty times forty bears and the following morning they all went to the Czar. The fox left all the bears in the courtyard and went inside alone, "Mighty Czar, I have come with a present from my master, Kuzma Getrich. He sends you forty times forty bears."

The Czar thanked the fox warmly, had the bears skinned and thought to himself, "This Kuzma Getrich must be a very rich fellow."

The fox returned to Kuzma and said, "Please roast me another hen, Kuzma. I really do promise to turn your luck."

Kuzma roasted the very last chicken, the fox gobbled it up and ran into the clearing to rest. A sable and a pine marten walked by and remarked, "Why are you sprawled here like this?"

"You too wouldn't be able to move, if you had been with me at the Czar's palace for lunch. I ate so much and drank so much, I thought my tummy would burst; and I am going again tomorrow."

"Please take us with you, fox," they pleaded.

"Why not? The Czar has more than enough food and drink; all you could want. Bring with you forty times forty sables and martens and we'll all go tomorrow."

They gathered together forty times forty sables and martens and the next morning they all went to the palace.

The fox left all the sables and martens in the courtyard and went to the Czar alone, "Mighty Czar, I have come to you with a gift from my master, Kuzma Getrich. The present he sends you is forty times forty sables and martens."

The Czar thanked the fox warmly, had the sables and martens skinned and said to himself, "This Kuzma Getrich must be a very, very rich fellow."

Once again the fox ran back to Kuzma Getrich, "Roast me another chicken, Kuzma,"

he cried. "I really promise to turn your luck." Kuzma grew angry this time, "You've already eaten my five hens. I have no more. And you haven't turned my luck!" he shouted.

"Stop worrying, Kuzma! I will keep my promise," the fox assured him, and trotted away back to the Czar, "Mighty Czar! My master, Kuzma Getrich, has sent me here to tell you he would like to court your daughter and ask for her hand in marriage."

"Of course he can court her," agreed the Czar. "I should be happy to give my daughter to such a rich man, such a gentleman. Go back and tell him to join me for lunch tomorrow."

The fox ran back to Kuzma Getrich. "The Czar has invited you for lunch tomorrow, Kuzma. He wants to give you his daughter in marriage," he said.

"But foxie, how can I go to the Czar's palace for lunch, when all I possess are these tatty old trousers?"

"Don't give that another thought, Kuzma. Just do what I tell you to, and you'll see, it will all come right," the fox promised.

The next morning Kuzma and the fox set out for the palace. The fox ran on ahead, Kuzma walked slowly behind. He was moaning, "How ashamed I shall be, when I get to the Czar in these tatty old pants."

In the meantime the fox came to the river and used his saw to cut through the bridge which spanned it. The moment Kuzma set his foot upon it, the bridge collapsed and he fell into the water. He very nearly drowned.

The fox ran to the Czar, "Oh, mighty Czar, what a dreadful thing has happened! The bridge has collapsed under Kuzma Getrich, all his golden coaches have floated away, and his servants have drowned. It is a miracle that Kuzma Getrich escaped with his bare life!"

The Czar immediately sent one of his gold coaches for Kuzma, putting inside an exquisite robe embroidered in gold, fashionable boots inlaid in silver and a sable hat strewn with pearls. When Kuzma put it all on, he looked just like a real prince. The Czar and his daughter could hardly take their eyes off him.

It seemed everything would end happily, for there was a great wedding of Kuzma Getrich and the Czar's daughter. The celebrations continued for three days. On the third day the Czar turned to Kuzma:

"Now, my dear son-in-law, we will go to your Czardom."

Kuzma Getrich was terribly worried and he said to the fox, "Alas, foxie, you promised to bring me good fortune, but it is turning into misfortune. Now the Czar will find out that all I possess is an old shack in the forest."

"Stop worrying, Kuzma! It will all have a happy ending."

The Czar, his daughter and Kuzma Getrich drove away from the palace in a gold carriage. The fox ran on ahead to show them the way. But instead of going towards Kuzma's shack in the woods, it went in the opposite direction.

The fox ran on and on, till it came to a green meadow, where shepherds were tending a huge flock of sheep.

THE GREEDY FOX
AND KUZMA GETRICH

"Tell me, shepherds," the fox called out to them, "Whose flock are you tending?"

"It is Czar Viper's flock."

"If you value your life, shepherds, say that this flock of sheep belongs to Kuzma Getrich. The Fiery Czar and his Flaming Czarina ride behind me and they could burn you to ashes.'

"Thank you, fox, for your good advice," cried the shepherds.

By then the gold carriage with Kuzma, the Czar and Czarina had arrived, and the Czar was asking, "Tell me, shepherds, to whom does this flock belong?"

"To Kuzma Getrich."

"You have excellent sheep, son-in-law," said the Czar with satisfaction, and they drove on.

In the meantime the fox came to some cowherds, who were tending a huge herd of cows.

"Tell me, cowherds," the fox called to them, "Whose herd are you looking after?"

"It is Czar Viper's herd."

"If you value your life, cowherds, say that this herd of cows belongs to Kuzma Getrich. The Fiery Czar and his Flaming Czarina ride behind me and they could burn you to ashes."

"Thank you, fox, for your good advice," cried the cowherds.

By then the gold carriage with Kuzma, the Czar and Czarina had arrived, and the the Czar was asking, "Tell me, cowherds, to whom does this herd belong?"

"To Kuzma Getrich."

"You have excellent cows, son-in-law," said the Czar with satisfaction, and they drove on.

In the meantime the fox came to some herdsmen who were tending a huge herd of horses.

"Tell me, herdsmen," the fox called to them, "Whose herd are you looking after?"

"It is Czar Viper's herd."

"If you value your life, say that this herd of horses belongs to Kuzma Getrich. The Fiery Czar and his Flaming Czarina ride behind me and they could burn you to ashes."

"Thank you, fox, for your good advice," cried the herdsmen.

Already the gold carriage with Kuzma, the Czar and Czarina had arrived and the Czar was asking:

"Tell me, herdsmen, to whom does this herd belong?"

"To Kuzma Getrich."

"You have fine horses, dear son-in-law," the Czar smiled contentedly.

The fox at last ran into the gold palace of Czar Viper and knocked on the gates.

Czar Viper stuck out all his seven dragon's heads and cried, "Who is knocking on my gates?"

The fox called loudly:

"Alas, Czar Viper, you're in trouble! The Fiery Czar and the Flaming Czarina ride behind me in a gold carriage. Run away as fast as you can, otherwise they will burn you to ashes."

As soon as Czar Viper heard this, he ran out of the gold palace and ran and ran, as fast as his legs could carry him. No one ever saw him again.

Shortly after the Czar arrived with his daughter and Kuzma Getrich by the palace gates. The fox was waiting to welcome them and the Czar could not stop marvelling at the splendid palace his son-in-law owned.

From that day on Kuzma lived happily in the gold palace with the Czar's daughter, and foxie, too. They roasted a big fat hen each day for their friend, and the greedy fox stayed with them, full and content.

THE TWELVE
MIKITAS

In a faraway land, where the goose thrashes the corn with its wings and the goat grinds the flour with its chin, there lived a merchant. He was so rich that caravans laden with his goods travelled over nine Czardoms; his own vessels sailed over nine oceans and he owned stores in nine distant towns.

This merchant had three sons. Two were clever and good and the third, Mikita, was wise and had a gallant heart.

The merchant built a new house for them all and said to his sons, "Remember your dreams during your first night in the new house. If you do, your dreams will come true."

The sons remembered. The eldest one dreamed that he was given a valiant mare, with reins edged in expensive fur. The saddle was of the rarest, softest leather, the stirrups lined with pure silk, and the crop studded with silver.

The father smiled and said, "This can easily come true," and he gave his son a valiant mare with all the trimmings, just as he had dreamed.

The second son dreamed that he owned a new robe, made of lovely velvet, with gold buttons as big as hazel nuts. There was a sable coat to go with the robe and high leather boots.

"This can easily come true," said the father and gave his second son exactly the same clothes as he had dreamed about.

"What was your dream?" he asked his youngest son. But he remained silent.

The father grew angry, and started to beat Mikita with a stick. But he remained silent. A traveller rode by and asked the merchant, "Why are you giving this lad a beating?"

"He is an ungrateful son. He refuses to tell me what he has dreamed about during the first night in our new house. That is why he is getting a beating."

"Sell me your son!" said the traveller.

"You can have him for nothing!" said the merchant in disgust and the traveller took the son and rode away.

On their journey he asked, "Tell me, Mikita, what was your dream during the first night in your new house?"

"I did not tell my father, so I won't tell you either," Mikita answered.

The traveller snatched a cane and started to beat the lad. The Czar rode by and asked, "Why are you beating this lad?"

"He is an ungrateful boy. He refuses to tell me what he dreamed about the first night in his new house."

"Sell me the boy!" said the Czar.

"You can have him for nothing, Czar!"

THE TWELVE MIKITAS

The Czar rode away towards the palace with Mikita. When they arrived, he asked, "Tell me, Mikita, what did you dream about during the first night in your new house?"

"I did not tell my father, I did not tell the traveller, so I won't tell you either."

The Czar grew very angry and gave orders for Mikita to be thrown into jail and to be fed only on crusts of bread and water.

Some time later the Czar prepared to visit a far distant land. It lay beyond three times nine mountains, three times nine forests and three times nine oceans. Twelve daughters of a Czar lived in this land and they were so alike, you could not tell them apart. They had the same hair, same voices, and the same faces of such rare beauty that it would be impossible to paint them or describe them. But only one of the twelve sisters was the one chosen by the Czar. She was the eldest one.

Time passes more slowly than it takes to tell a story. So one year, two years, three years passed and the Czar was still on his travels — no one had seen him, nor heard of him. Poor Mikita was still in prison, fed only on crusts of bread and water. In the end the Czar's sister, beautiful Vasilisa, who was left in the palace, asked that Mikita be brought to her and said, "Please advise me what to do, dear Mikita. The Czar has gone away, and I have heard nothing of him for three years now. It is as if the ground had opened up and swallowed him up."

Mikita said, "If you permit, Czarina, I will borrow a horse, a sword and a gun and will search for the Czar."

The Czarina agreed, smiled at Mikita sweetly, and he chose a horse, a sword and a gun and was off.

He rode on and on, till he reached a sunny meadow where there was a nest of snakes. He was just about to bid his horse to trample them with its hooves, when the largest of the snakes rose and spoke to Mikita in a human voice, "Do not bid your valiant horse to trample us to death with its hooves. You would be wiser to give us your horse in exchange for seven mile boots."

Mikita gave his horse to the snakes and took the seven mile boots. He put them on and with every step crossed seven miles.

It took only a short time to cross the three times nine mountains. In a stump of a tree beyond, he found a hive of bees. Mikita was just about to cut the stump with his sword and eat the sweet honey, when the largest bee flew out of it and said in a human voice, "Do not cut this tree stump with your sword. You would be wiser to give us your sword in exchange for a magic cap. Anyone who puts this cap on becomes invisible."

Mikita exchanged his sword for the magic cap, and continued on his journey. Each step covered seven miles and so only a short time later he had crossed the three times nine forests, and found himself by the sea. There were twelve storks sitting near the shore.

Mikita thought he could shoot them with his gun and rost them for his dinner. He was getting very hungry. But the biggest stork flew overhead and called to Mikita in a human voice, "Do not shoot us with your gun, Mikita. You would be wiser to give us the gun in exchange for my eleven stork-brothers. Then there would be twelve of you and you would be stronger."

Mikita gave the stork his gun and was given the eleven stork-brothers in return. The minute the storks stepped on the shore, they changed into strong youths as like Mikita as peas in a pod. They had the same hair, same voices, same clothes and the same names. They were all called Mikita! These Mikitas were all nice lads, they ate well, drank well, slept well, laughed a lot, and were kind and good.

Mikita the merchant's son put all the eleven other Mikitas on his back and walked on. Each step covered seven miles, so only a short while later he had crossed the three times nine seas and reached the distant shore. The Czar's ship came in to dock at the very same time.

The Czar was overjoyed to see the twelve able helpers, and was not in the least vexed that Mikita was no longer shut in jail, chewing hard crusts and sipping plain water.

They set out immediately for the town where the twelve Czarinas reigned.

All the sisters were jolly and gay and would have liked to get married, except the eldest one. It was just this one that the Czar had chosen for himself. Because of her, all the others waited on and on, hoping she would fall in love and would want to marry. Then they could marry too.

Their palace was really magnificent. The walls were of white marble, the windows of clear crystal, the gates and doors of solid oak and the turrets were made from pure gold. In front of the palace stood one hundred poles, and on ninety-nine of them were the severed heads of hopeful bridegrooms, whom the eldest sister had refused. The hundredth pole was the only empty one.

The Czar entered the palace, stepped before the sisters, bowed deeply and said:

"Beautiful daughters of the Czar, I have come because I have chosen one of you for my bride and I want to ask for her hand in marriage."

The sisters asked, "Which one of us have you chosen for your bride?"

"The eldest one."

"Very well then," said the eldest sister. "Come back tomorrow morning. If you will pick me out from all my other sisters, I will marry you. But if you fail to recognize me, you will be shorter by the head. I will have your head stuck on the remaining pole in front of my palace."

The Czar grew sad and went to Mikita, the merchant's son, to seek advice.

"How can I be happy, when I have been told I must pick out my bride from her sisters. They are all as alike as peas in a pod; the same hair, same voices, the same wonderful beauty. If I recognize her, she will take me for a husband, but if I do not, I will be shorter by the head."

"We will think of something by tomorrow," Mikita consoled him. Then he put the magic cap on his own head, and immediately became invisible. He went to the palace of the twelve sisters. Mikita walked through all the courtyards, all the halls and rooms, and in the very last one he found the twelve sisters talking to one another. One of them was saying: "Tomorrow yet another bridegroom will lose his head."

Another one said:

"It is a shame really, for he is very handsome and is a Czar of a mighty and a rich Czardom."

Another sister, the eldest one, smiled, "If the Czar only knew what he does not know, he would not have to lose his head."

"If he knew what?" asked the others.

"If he knew that tomorrow morning, when he will be trying to pick me out amongst you, I shall be the third from the left. Then he would recognize me."

Mikita listened to all this carefully, then went away.

In the morning he went with all the other Mikitas and the Czar to the palace for the picking of the princess. All the sisters stood in a row, alike as peas in a pod — the same voice, the same hair — how could he choose the right one? But Mikita whispered in the Czar's ear:

"The third from the left is the one you want."

The Czar walked over to the third maiden and took her by the hand. She was the right one. Everyone was happy that he guessed correctly. The Czar was overjoyed to have gained a bride instead of losing his head; Mikita was happy, because he gave the Czar such good advice; the other eleven Mikitas were happy too, because they liked to be happy; the eleven younger sisters were happy, because they thought their eldest one would marry at last and then they, too, could look for bridegrooms. They already had their eyes on the Mikitas. No wonder, too, for they were handsome youths and would have made suitable bridegrooms. The eldest sister seemed happy too. She smiled sweetly at the Czar and prepared to hold a great feast.

But all this was really pretence. The eldest sister was actually absolutely furious, because at last she had met her match. She suspected that the Czar did not pick her out on his own, for she noticed how Mikita lent across and whispered in his ear. She wanted to have her revenge, but she had no idea which one of the twelve Mikitas was the real one.

The feast ended late at night and they all went to bed. When everyone was asleep, the eldest sister went into the room where all the Mikitas were resting. They were sleeping in white feather beds, their hands folded behind their heads, snoring loudly. The eldest sister said:

"The eldest sister was the third from the right."

"No, she was the third from the left," mumbled Mikita the merchant's son in his sleep, and gave himself away. The maiden tiptoed to his bed, took his left shoe and went away.

When in the morning Mikita woke up, he was surprised to see that his left shoe had disappeared. Suspecting that something nasty might happen, he hid all the left shoes of all the other Mikitas too. When they all assembled round the breakfast table, the eldest sister entered, saying:

"I found a shoe yesterday. Does it belong to one of you?"

All the Mikitas were shouting that it must be theirs, for they all had their left shoe missing. The eldest sister frowned; she was even more furious. She turned to the Czar:

"As you recognized me yesterday from among my sisters, I will take you for a husband. But first you must bring me tomorrow morning, one of the pair of special wedding shoes. If you don't succeed, you will lose your head."

The sad Czar turned to Mikita once again for advice.

"Things can't be that bad, we'll think of something by tomorrow," Mikita consoled him when he heard about the Czar's latest task. He put the magic cap on his head and immediately became invisible. Then he went to find the sisters.

As he was walking along a passage, he met the eldest sister who was hurrying out of the palace. Mikita followed. The maiden ran through the town, along narrow back streets, till she came to a tiny cottage at the very edge of the town. Mikita was following close behind her. An old cobbler lived in the cottage. The princess said to him, "Cobbler, I want you to make me a shoe from green silk, a shoe embroidered with pearls, studded in diamonds, with the front so round that an egg could roll right round it, and the heel so high a sparrow could fly under it.

The cobbler did as he was asked. When the shoe was finished, the waiting, invisible Mikita snatched it and was off. As the cobbler did not see him, he did not realize straight away that the shoe had disappeared. When he noticed it had gone, he searched and searched, but all in vain. There was nothing else to do but to make another shoe!

The following morning the Czar and all the Mikitas went once again to see the sisters. The eldest one was waiting with the green silk shoe in her hand. She passed it over to the Czar. At that moment Mikita slipped the other shoe into the Czar's hand, the one he took from the cobbler the previous night — and so the Czar had a pair.

Everyone was overjoyed that the Czar had fulfilled the second task. The eldest sister also seemed overjoyed. She smiled sweetly at the Czar and once again organized a lavish feast. But in reality she was absolutely furious, because once again Mikita proved cleverer than her. Of course she had noticed that he passed the second shoe to the Czar. How pleased she would be if she could revenge herself, but she had no idea which of the twelve Mikitas was the real one.

When the feast was over and everyone was asleep, the princess tiptoed once again into the room where all the Mikitas were resting in their white feather beds, and said:

"The shoe to match the other from the pair is made from red silk, and is embroidered in gold, and studded in silver."

"No," spoke Mikita, the merchant's son, "It is made from green silk, embroidered with pearls, studded with diamonds."

The maiden realized he was the real Mikita. She crept to his bed and cut a lock of hair off his forehead. Then she tiptoed away.

When Mikita awoke the following morning, he was surprised to see that a lock of his hair had been cut off. Rising quickly, he cut an identical lock off the other Mikita's hair. When at breakfast time the eldest sister saw them all with a lock of hair missing, she frowned and was even more furious. She said to the Czar, "As you picked me out from my sisters, as you brought me the shoe to match the other of the wedding pair, I agree to take you for a husband. But first bring me the gold wedding ring, which hangs on the highest branch of a green oak tree in a deserted field set in the middle of a dense forest beyond the nine mountains. I want to have it by tomorrow morning. If you don't succeed, you will lose your head."

The sad Czar turned to Mikita for advice.

"Don't be afraid, dear Czar, we'll think of something this time, too," Mikita consoled him. Putting on his seven mile boots, and his magic cap, he set forth on the journey. As with each step he travelled seven miles, he soon crossed the nine mountains and found himself in the deserted field in the middle of the dense forest, right under the green oak. On the highest branch of the tree the gold ring was hanging.

"There's plenty of time, so I might as well take a nap," Mikita said to himself. He lay down in the grass and fell fast asleep. He slept on and on, right till the evening, right through the night; the dawn broke and he was still asleep.

The palace of the twelve sisters was far from peaceful! The time had come for the Czar to go to his princess, but there was no sign of Mikita or of the gold ring. The Czar went to talk to the other Mikitas, but they were hopeless! They were good lads, they ate well, drank well, slept well, laughed a lot, they were willing and kind, but knew nothing else. They did not know the whereabouts of Mikita, the merchant's son, or of the gold ring. The Czar was broken-hearted, for he knew he would lose his head and the princess too. But what could he do? He bade the brothers a sad goodbye and went to the princess, knowing he would be facing his own death, which would bring grief to his beautiful sister, Vasilisa.

But the eleven Mikitas were not quite helpless. They went out and ran to the sea, jumped into the waves and as soon as their bodies touched the water, they turned into white storks. They flew on and on, over three times nine oceans, till they came to their eldest brother, who had exchanged them for Mikita's gun. Perhaps this brother could advise them.

When the eldest stork had listened to everything, he thought a while, then took a pair of binoculars from under his wings and looked through them beyond the sea and mountains to the deserted field in the dense forest. At last he saw the green oak tree, the highest branch, and on it the gold ring. He did not see Mikita. How could he see him, when Mikita had the magic cap on his head and was invisible! The stork was very upset and said, "If Mikita, the merchant's son, cannot have the ring, neither can anyone else!"

Taking Mikita's gun, he aimed and fired, and shot the gold ring from the highest branch. The eleven storks, the eleven Mikitas, returned with heavy hearts to the palace of the twelve sisters.

They did not know that when the eldest stork shot down the gold ring from the highest branch, it fell right on Mikita's nose! This woke Mikita up. He gazed round him in a daze; on the ground he saw the gold ring, in the sky he saw the gold sun. Realizing it was already dawn, he remembered that the Czar should have given the gold ring to the eldest sister. Hurriedly he took the ring and sped to the palace of the twelve sisters. With each step he crossed seven miles, so it did not take long to travel over the nine mountains and to find himself on the forecourt of the palace. He jumped with both feet through the window into the room where the Czar and the twelve sisters were gathered. The crystal glass broke into thousands of pieces, but no one knew how, because Mikita was still wearing his magic cap. Only the Czar felt an object being pressed into his hand. He took a look, and there it was, the gold ring!

Everyone rejoiced that the Czar after all found the gold wedding ring for the princess. The eldest sister also seemed happy; she smiled sweetly at the Czar and once again held a grand feast. But all that was pure pretence. Actually she was fuming with anger. When the celebrations were over and everyone retired to bed, the princess returned to the room where all the Mikitas slept and said, "The gold ring was hanging on a birch tree, on the lowest branch."

"No," said Mikita, the merchant's son. "It was hanging on a branch of an oak tree, on the highest one."

The princess realized this was the real Mikita. She tiptoed to his side and bit him on the nose. Her teeth were like pearls and they marked the nose beautifully. Then she went away.

When the next morning Mikita awoke, he saw that the princess had bitten his nose. He rose quickly and wanted to bite the noses of all the other Mikitas, but alas! The princess and her sisters were the only ones with such tiny, sharp teeth like pearls.

"There's nothing else for it, brothers," said Mikita, the merchant's son. "You must run to the younger sisters and ask them to bite your noses too. Otherwise you and I will be in danger!"

The Mikitas hurried to the sisters, and at breakfast they all sat down with bitten noses, beautifully marked with pearly teeth. When the eldest sister saw this, she frowned like thunder, but what could she do? She realized that she had really met her match in Mikita and that she would not get the better of him.

So a splendid wedding was held. All the twelve sisters married at the same time. The eldest one wed her Czar and the others wed the eleven Mikitas, of course! But the twelfth Mikita, the merchant's son, he remained single.

"Don't feel left out," the Czar consoled him. "When we return home, I will give you my sister, the lovely Vasilisa, and you too will have a splendid wedding. I will also give you half my Czardom."

When the wedding festivities were over, the eleven sisters and the eleven Mikitas stayed on in their own Czardom. Mikita, the merchant's son, put the eldest sister and the

Czar onto his back, and in his seven mile boots covered the distance in no time at all; they crossed the three times nine oceans, the three times nine forests, the tree times nine mountains and were home.

So another wedding was held, just as splendid as the first. This was the marriage of the beautiful Vasilisa and of Mikita, the merchant's son, who was also given half the Czardom. Mikita, of course, invited his father and his brothers to the wedding, and they were pleased to see his good fortune. The father begged Mikita's forgiveness for having treated him so badly.

The wedding celebrations went on for a whole week. At the end of the last day the twelve most respected elders from all the Czardom came to the palace. They bathed Mikita's feet in a golden bowl, then everyone went to bed.

In the night the old merchant, Mikita's father, woke with a terrible thirst. He saw the golden bowl and drank the water which was in it. It was the same water that the elders had used to bathe Mikita's feet.

The next day the father said to Mikita, "Can you tell me now, son, what you dreamt about that first night in our new house?"

Mikita smiled, "I dreamt I should become a Czar, that my feet would be bathed in a golden bowl and that you, father, would drink the water from that bowl."

Now this really is the end of the story.

THE STUPID WOLF

This all happened when the billy-goat was a policeman, the sparrow a minister and the cockerel a police warden. The aged eagle was the Czar and he ruled very wisely.

The wolf came to the eagle, bowed deeply, and complained, "Mighty Czar, I am so hungry I could cry! Give me something to eat."

"Why should I feed you? As a wolf, it is up to you to do your own hunting."

"At least tell me, mighty Czar, what I should hunt."

"See that filly over there? Go and eat it up!"

The wolf thanked the Czar eagle and went to eat the filly.

"I am going to gobble you up, filly!"

"Why is that?" asked the mare.

"The Czar eagle ordered me to do so."

"How could he have given you such an order! I have the Czar's stamp on me, so you cannot eat me up."

"Where is this stamp?"

"On this back leg," said the filly, raising her foot.

The wolf began examining it, looking for the stamp. At that moment the filly kicked him hard, straight in the mouth and knocked him over.

When the wolf came to, the filly had galloped away.

The wolf returned to the Czar eagle. "Mighty Czar, I am so hungry I could cry! Give me something to eat."

"But I gave you permission to eat the filly."

"That filly was nasty; it kicked me in the mouth and ran away."

"Very well then. Go and eat the ram which is grazing over there!"

The wolf thanked the Czar eagle and went after the ram.

"Ram, I'm going to gobble you up!"

"Why should you gobble me up?"

"The Czar eagle told me to do so."

"Which end are you going to start from, head or tail?"

"I don't mind. What do you think?"

"It is better to start with the head. I tell you what; stand over that gorge over there, open your mouth wide and I will jump right into it."

The wolf placed himself over the gorge, closed his eyes and opened his mouth wide. The ram ran down the slope from above and pushed the wolf down the gorge with its horns.

The wolf fell until he reached the very bottom.

When the wolf came to and clawed his way out of the gorge, the ram was gone. So he returned to the Czar eagle, complaining, "Mighty Czar, I am so hungry I could cry! Give me something to eat."

"But I gave you permission to eat the ram."

"The ram was nasty; it pushed me down the gorge with its horns and ran off."

"Very well then. Do you see that tailor over there? Go and eat him up! But don't come back here again! Otherwise I will tell billy-goat policeman and cockerel the warden to throw you in jail."

"Tailor, I am going to gobble you up!"

"Why should you gobble me up?"

"The Czar eagle told me to do so."

"Oh well, that is a different matter! Come on then, doggie, gobble me up!"

The wolf was angry.

"I am not a dog, I am a wolf!"

"So you are a wolf? You're a very small wolf. Come here a minute, let me measure you."

The tailor took a tape measure and started measuring the wolf, first from tail to head, then from head to tail.

"I don't seem to be able to get it right. This tail of yours is in the way. I'll have to cut it off."

Before the wolf had a chance to move, the tailor took out his scissors and with a single cut robbed the wolf of his tail.

The wolf howled with pain and ran away. Where could he run to though, when Czar eagle forbade him to return?

He ran to his brother wolves instead.

"Where did you leave your tail, brother?" they asked.

"The tailor was measuring me and he cut it off, because it was in his way."

The wolves went after the tailor to gobble him up, because he cut off the tail of their brother. When the tailor saw the danger, he climbed up a tree.

The wolves ran under the tree and called to the tailor, "Come down at once, tailor! We have come to gobble you up, because you dared to cut off the tail of our brother."

But the tailor refused to come down.

"I prefer to stay up here. Just come and get me!"

The wolves jumped and jumped as high as they could, but it was not high enough. The tailless wolf then said, "I have an idea, brothers. I'll stand under the tree, and you climb on to each others backs, on top of me. Then we will reach the tailor."

The wolves climbed on the back of the tailless one, one on top of the other. The highest one was just about to get the tailor, when the tailor remarked, "Come on then, wolfie, I'll measure you too!"

As soon as the tailless wolf at the bottom heard that the tailor was preparing to measure once again, he was so frightened that he jumped up and ran away. The other wolves fell in a heap, and as soon as they got on their feet, they ran after him.

The tailor in the tree laughed and laughed till he got hiccups. And as he hiccupped, he lost his balance, fell off the tree, picked himself up and went home.

Our wolf runs around without its tail to this day, afraid to go to Czar eagle, afraid of what he'd have to say.

UNCLE NAUMA

Here is another story. If you listen attentively, whether you are young or old, I will give you a sable fur and a pretty maiden, one hundred roubles for your wedding and fifty extra.

Once there was a Czar who had twelve huntsmen. For six days a week they hunted for the Czar, roaming the woods, shooting sable and deer, wild geese and swans. Anything they caught on the seventh day, they could keep for themselves. The youngest of the huntsmen was called Andrew. When he was hunting for the Czar, he always shot many animals, but when, on the seventh day, he was hunting for himself, he could hardly catch a squirrel, or shoot a quail.

One day Andrew was in the forest on the seventh day and, as usual, caught nothing. As he was returning sadly home, he noticed a white dove at the edge of the forest sitting in a tree.

"I will shoot the dove at least," he thought, took aim with his bow and caught the bird in its wing.

The dove fell to the ground and said to Andrew, "Spare me, Andrew, and take me home with you. Sit me on your window, knock me to the floor and you will see what will happen. Then you can either keep me, or send me away."

Andrew took the dove home, sat it on the window sill, knocked it down and — lo and behold — a beautiful maiden stood before him, more beautiful than anyone he had ever seen or heard of. Her name was Beautiful Doe.

"I could never send away such a beautiful girl. I will keep her for myself," huntsman Andrew decided.

After that he lived happily with Beautiful Doe in his cottage.

Some time later Beautiful Doe said to Andrew, "Don't you think we are rather badly off?"

"Yes and no," answered Andrew. "On the six days I hunt for the Czar I am the best hunter. But on the seventh, when I hunt for myself, I hardly catch anything."

"Never mind," said Doe. "Borrow one hundred roubles from somewhere and buy some silk with it."

Andrew visited all his friends. From some he borrowed just a rouble, from others five at a time.

When he had one hundred roubles, he bought the silk and took it to Doe. The maiden sewed the most exquisite rug from the silk, with a map of all the Czardom: towns and villages, forests and fields, birds in the sky, animals on the land and fish in the water. The sun, the moon and the stars circled round.

"Take this rug to sell at the market," Beautiful Doe told Andrew. "But do not ask a certain price, let whoever wants it decide."

Andrew took the rug and went to the market. Many merchants examined it, but no one could decide how much such work and beauty was worth. In the end the Czar's councillor came to the market and he said to Andrew:

"I will give you ten thousand roubles for this rug."

"Very well," agreed Andrew, took the ten thousand roubles, paid his debts and brought the rest back to Doe.

The Czar's councillor took the rug to the palace and showed it to the Czar.

"Sell me that rug for twenty thousand roubles!" said the Czar.

"It is yours," agreed the councillor and went to Andrew to order another rug.

When the councillor arrived at Andrew's cottage he knocked on the door, Beautiful Doe opened it. The councillor stepped over the door-step with one foot, but he never crossed it with the other foot! He was thunderstruck by such loveliness and dumbfounded, too. He could not utter a single word, so Doe pushed him out again.

After that the Czar's councillor was listless and dreamy-eyed, unable to think of anything but the lovely wife of Andrew.

The Czar noticed this and said to his councillor:

"What is the matter with you these days, councillor?"

"What is the matter, gracious Czar? From the day my eyes fell on the wife of the hunter Andrew, I can think of nothing else but her beauty."

The Czar was surprised to hear this and decided he must see Beautiful Doe for himself. He dressed in peasant's robes and went to Andrew's cottage. When he knocked on the door, Beautiful Doe answered. The Czar stepped over the threshold with one foot, but the other did not follow. He was so dumbfounded by such beauty, he could not utter a single word, so Doe pushed him out, too.

After that the Czar was listless and dreamy-eyed, thinking of nothing else except how he could take the Beautiful Doe away from Andrew. One day he said to his councillor, "You are, after all, my councillor, so think of some task for huntsman Andrew, which will take him far away and keep him away for ever."

The councillor thought and thought, and went on thinking, but could not think of any ideas. As he was thinking, he went to the inn, where a shabby beggar came to sit next to him.

"Leave me alone! Go and sit elsewhere," the Czar's councillor shouted.

The beggar only smiled and said, "Don't chase me away, dear sir! Order me a mug of beer instead, for I may be able to help you."

The Czar's councillor ordered a mug of ale for the beggar and told him his problems.

"They are easy to solve," the beggar assured him. "Send hunter Andrew for the sheep with the golden fleece. He will find it on a copper island in the middle of the ocean, tied to a silver pole. When this lamb bleats, everyone within a hundred miles will start to laugh."

UNCLE NAUMA

"What a splendid idea," chuckled the Czar's councillor and rushed back to his master.

The very next day the Czar asked to see huntsman Andrew and said to him, "Good hunter Andrew, I need your help. Bring me the sheep with the golden fleece, which is tied to a silver pole on a copper island in the middle of the ocean. When this lamb bleats, everyone within a hundred miles starts to laugh. If you bring me this sheep, I will give you one thousand roubles, but do not dare to return empty handed!"

Hunter Andrew was very worried, but he could not refuse. He returned sadly home.

"Are you troubled?" asked Beautiful Doe.

"Of course I am troubled, for the Czar has given me an impossible task! I am to bring him the sheep with the golden fleece, which is tied to a silver pole on a copper island in the middle of the ocean. When this lamb bleats, everyone within one hundred miles starts to laugh. If I bring it, I will receive one thousand roubles, but I must not return empty handed."

Beautiful Doe smiled and said, "This is not an impossible task, but an easy one! Go to sleep now, everything always seems better in the morning."

When Andrew was in a deep sleep, Doe took out her embroidered scarf and waved it. Straight away a huge toad appeared and asked, "What is your wish, Beautiful Doe?"

Doe replied, "Granny toad, please bring me the sheep with the golden fleece, which is tied to a silver pole on a copper island in the middle of the ocean. When this lamb bleats, everyone within one hundred miles starts to laugh."

Granny toad said nothing, just croaked to herself, "Why does Beautiful Doe wake me from my sleep for such a trifle?"

Then the toad hopped away.

Granny toad returned before sunrise with the lamb with the golden fleece. The happy Andrew took it to the Czar.

The Czar paid him the thousand roubles, sent the lamb to the palace yard, and ordered his councillor to think of a harder task for Andrew.

The councillor did not bother to think, but hurried back to the inn and related what happened to the shabby beggar. When he had given him a mug of beer, the beggar said, "So Andrew found the lamb! Send him then for the tom-cat sleep-sender, which is tied to a gold pole on a silver island in the middle of the ocean. When this cat miaows, everyone within one hundred miles falls asleep."

The councillor did not even thank the beggar but hastened to the Czar.

The next day the Czar summoned huntsman Andrew and said, "Dear huntsman Andrew, I need your help once again. Bring me the tom-cat sleep-sender, which is tied to a gold pole on a silver island in the middle of the ocean. When this cat miaows, everyone within one hundred miles falls asleep. If you succeed, I will give you two thousand roubles, but do not dare to return empty handed!"

The troubled hunter Andrew returned sadly to Beautiful Doe and told her everything. She dismissed his worries with a wave of her hand and sent him to bed. Then, taking out her embroidered scarf, she summoned the huge toad once again, who asked, "What is your wish, Beautiful Doe?"

Doe said, "Granny toad, please bring me tom-cat sleep-sender, which is tied to a gold pole on a silver island in the middle of the ocean. When this cat miaows, everyone within one hundred miles falls asleep."

Granny toad hopped away, croaking to herself, "Why does Beautiful Doe wake me for such a trifle?"

Before sunrise she had returned with tom-cat sleep-sender.

When Andrew gave tom-cat sleep-sender to the Czar, he was paid two thousand roubles and the cat was put in the palace yard. The Czar called the councillor and said, "Once again Andrew has fulfilled his task. Unless you can think of one that he cannot accomplish, get out of my sight for ever!"

The worried councillor went to the inn and complained to the shabby beggar, how badly he had advised him. The beggar thought a while, drank one mug of ale, then another and yet a third, and then said, "I have it! Tell Andrew to go there, I don't know where, and to bring that, I don't know what. Surely he can't fulfil this task!"

The delighted councillor rushed back to the Czar who was very content with the idea. Immediately he sent for hunter Andrew and said, "Dear huntsman Andrew, I need your help just once again. Hurry there, I don't know where, and bring me that, I don't know what. If you succeed, I will give you three hundred thousand roubles, but do not dare to return empty-handed!

Andrew sauntered happily home. He thought this would be an easy task for Beautiful Doe to accomplish. But Doe grew sad and said, "Dear Andrew, this is not a simple task, but a most difficult one."

Taking the embroidered scarf, she summoned Granny toad and said, "Granny toad, do you think you could go there, I don't know where, and bring me that, I don't know what?"

Granny toad thought hard and sighed, "This is indeed a most difficult task, Beautiful Doe. I could not manage it on my own. Andrew, get on my back and I will take you there, I don't know where, for that, I don't know what."

Andrew looked at the toad worriedly. "I would squash you if I sat on you!" he said.

But the toad was not worried. "Don't be afraid, and sit!" she ordered.

Hunter Andrew then sat on Granny toad's back and the toad started to inhale air; she grew till she was the size of a horse. Then she began to hop. With the first leap the toad leapt out of town, with the second leap she hopped over the black forest and with the third leap she hopped over the wide field. So the toad hopped and hopped until they reached the ocean. Then, with one mighty leap they landed on the copper island, where the sheep with the golden fleece had been tied to the silver pole; another mighty leap brought them to the silver island, where the tom-cat sleep-sender had once been tied to the golden pole; the last mighty leap brought them to a gold island. There the toad said, "I must leave you here, dear hunter Andrew. Now you must help yourself, for I cannot help you further. Go where your feet take you, follow your eyes, go there, I don't know where, and you will find that, I don't know what."

Then Granny toad hopped away.

Andrew went where his feet led him, he went there, I don't know where, till he came to a cottage, but it was not a cottage; he entered a room, but it was not a room and hid behind the stove, but it was not a stove. As he sat behind the stove, a skinny man walked in, with whiskers down to his elbows; he sat at the table and cried, "Uncle Nauma, I wish to eat!"

As quick as a flash the table was laden with food; there was so much to eat, delicious roast beef, with a knife of sharp steel and a whole barrel of wine. The skinny man started to eat greedily, cutting the meat off with the knife, downing it with the green wine. Soon there was nothing left but bare bones and an empty barrel. Then he shouted, "Uncle Nauma, clear the table!"

Straight away everything had disappeared and the skinny man went away.

Andrew thought he could try this magic too, so he cried, "Please Uncle Nauma, could you give me something to eat?"

In a flash the table was laden with food. There was all he could wish for. Andrew had never seen such a feast. He sat down at the table and said, "Uncle Nauma, come and sit with me, then we can eat together."

A voice boomed nearby, "Thank you, good fellow! I have been serving now for one thousand years, but no one has ever invited me to share even a crust of bread. But you have invited me to share a feast."

Andrew was amazed to see the meat invisibly sliced and eaten, the goblets invisibly filled and emptied. When they had both had enough, Andrew said, "Let me see you now, Uncle Nauma!"

The voice replied, "I can't do that. You see I am — I don't know what."

"You are the very person I have been sent to find!" cried Andrew joyfully and told Uncle Nauma what he had come for.

"Do not worry, I will return with you," Uncle Nauma said. "Give me to the Czar, but you shall be my only master. This is because you are the only kind person I have met during one thousand years.

With that Uncle Nauma took Andrew over the ocean, over the wide fields, over the black forest, right to the Czar's palace.

The Czar was surprised to see Andrew back so soon, especially empty handed. Andrew assured him, "Mighty Czar! I went I don't know where, and I have brought you I don't know what. But it will fulfil your every wish. Am I right?"

"You are perfectly right," confirmed the invisible voice.

"If this is true, then fetch Beautiful Doe, the wife of hunter Andrew!" cried the Czar. No sooner said than done — and the lovely Doe stood before them.

"And now take hunter Andrew to the other side of the world, so he could never return!" the Czar shouted.

As soon as he had spoken, the Czar himself disappeared, as if the earth had opened and swallowed him up, and his nasty councillor too.

"They are now both on the other side of the world and they will never come back again," said the voice of Uncle Nauma.

As a Czardom cannot be without a Czar, the people made Andrew into their Czar and Beautiful Doe their Czarina. They certainly could not have a better ruler, when Uncle Nauma served him so faithfully!

UNCLE NAUMA

THE CRAFTY FARMER
AND THE BEAR AND THE FOX

Once there was a farmer who was so crafty, he had more brains in his heel than others have in their heads.

One day when he was ploughing his field a bear came by and said, "Farmer, I am going to eat you up, farmer."

"Wait, bear, you shouldn't do that!" replied the farmer. "I will make it up to you. I will sow beet in this field. When it ripens, I will give you everything except the roots."

The bear agreed.

The farmer sowed the beet, and it soon ripened. The farmer dug it out, gave the bear the leaves and kept the roots for himself. He took them to the market and sold them at a profit.

The bear realized the crafty farmer had got the better of him and said, "I will eat you after all."

"Don't do that, bear," begged the farmer. "I am just about to sow some wheat. When it ripens, you can have the roots and I'll just have the tops."

The bear agreed.

The wheat grew and the farmer harvested it. He sold the corn on the market for a large sum, and covered his roof with the straw. He told the bear to come and get the roots when he had ploughed the stubble.

The bear realized that once again the farmer had got the better of him, and he was very angry. "This time I really will eat you up."

"If it has to be, it has to be," sighed the farmer. "But let me finish ploughing the stubble."

The bear agreed and went into the wood to take a nap.

A fox trotted by and asked the farmer, "Why are you so sad, farmer?"

"Who wouldn't be sad? The bear is waiting for me in the woods. As soon as I finish ploughing, he will eat me up."

"Things may not be so bad," the fox consoled him. "What will you give me if I get rid of the bear?"

"I will give you two chickens," promised the farmer.

"Agreed! Now leave it to me," said the fox and ran off.

When the farmer finished ploughing, the bear waddled to his side, ready to gobble him up. At that moment the fox appeared on the edge of the woods. It was shouting to the farmer, "I am hunting bears and wolves! Have you seen any?"

The bear was terribly frightened. He squatted down behind the farmer's cart and begged. "Say you haven't seen any, farmer!"

The farmer said exactly that, but the fox was not satisfied.

THE CRAFTY FARMER
           AND THE BEAR AND THE FOX

"What is that, behind your cart?"

"Say it is a tree trunk," said the bear.

The farmer said exactly that, but the fox was not satisfied.

"If it was a tree trunk, you would tie it on the cart. I think I'll have a closer look."

The bear begged the farmer to hurry up and tie him up on the cart, before the fox got to them.

The farmer did exactly that, just before the fox arrived. The fox looked at the bear and shook its head.

"What a strange tree trunk. If it was a real tree trunk, an axe would be wedged in it."

So the farmer took the axe, drove it into the bear and killed him.

"Now, dear farmer, give me the two chickens," said the fox.

"Yes, of course," agreed the farmer. "Come back to my cottage with me."

The fox went. When they arrived at the cottage, the farmer opened the front door and an enormous dog jumped at the fox. The fox ran away as fast as its legs would carry it with the dog hot on its heels. The farmer laughed and laughed, till tears trickled down his cheeks, at how he managed to cheat even the sly fox.

The fox was glad to escape with its life.

And I am glad that we have come to the end of the story and I can have a rest.

CZAR EAGLE

The gnat and the fly had a quarrel. The fly bit the gnat, the gnat nipped the mosquito, the mosquito bit the cow, the cow trod on the sparrow. All the insects, birds and beasts started to fight until it grew into the great animal war. They all fought for a whole week; then they all went home again. That is, all but the eagle, who stayed perched in the tree, for his wing was broken.

Ivan the merchant's son went by and saw the eagle in the tree. He was just about to shoot the bird, when the eagle spoke in a human voice, "Ivan the merchant's son, do not shoot me! I am a man just like yourself, but I am under a wicked spell. Take me home with you, feed me, nurse me for a year and a day, and you will see I will bring you good fortune and happiness."

Ivan the merchant's son took the eagle home. He nursed him and fed him well. The eagle had an enormous appetite; each day he ate half of a ram.

The old merchant was not very happy to see the eagle devour so many rams. He was indeed an expensive lodger. He said to his son, "Son, give that eagle away, or he will eat us out of the house."

But the son would not hear of it, and, as he was an only child, this time he got his own way.

Some time later the old merchant was angry once again because the eagle was eating so many rams. While Ivan was out, he took the eagle to the woods and threw him down the gorge. No one knew about this, except the old cook, and she told Ivan.

Ivan the merchant's son went to the gorge and rescued the bird. He took the eagle to a shepherd who was tending a flock of sheep nearby, and asked the shepherd to feed and nurse him, and he would repay him well.

Eleven months and a day went by when the old merchant heard that the shepherd was looking after the eagle and his own son was paying him for it. He was so angry he ordered his son to leave home.

The merchant's son ran to the eagle, sobbing wildly, and told him what had happened. The eagle said, "Let us see, perhaps I am already strong enough and well fed enough. Take me by my wings and shake me as hard as you can, until my eagle skin comes off."

The merchant's son took the eagle by his wings, shook him hard, until a pair of human legs came out of the skin. Ivan had no more strength left.

"Rest a while and try again, perhaps then you will be able to shake off the remains of the eagle skin."

After he had rested, Ivan took the eagle by his wings and shook him with all his might. A human trunk and a head came out of the skin, but by then Ivan was exhausted.

"Have another rest. I know it is hard work. It would have been easier if I had rested and had been fed for yet another month. Never mind, perhaps you'll manage to shake out my arms this time. We shall both be in trouble if you don't succeed."

Ivan the merchant's son rested a while, then, taking the eagle by his wings, he shook him so hard that the skin came off the arms and hands, except for the little finger of the left hand. Ivan took his knife and cut the little finger off. A most handsome youth, Czar Eagle, stood before him.

Thank you, Ivan, for setting me free. It was wise of you to cut off my little finger. Let us embrace each other to seal our friendship."

They embraced and kissed, then set out into the world to seek their fortune. They travelled far and wide, across plains and forests, until they came to a large, beautiful town. Czar Eagle said to Ivan the merchant's son:

"Go to a certain house in this town and ask the lady of the house for the gold key to the cellar."

The merchant's son went to the certain house and asked the lady for the gold key to the cellar. She seemed startled and said, "It must be my brother Czar Eagle who sends you here. I have not seen him for ten years now, and I don't need to see him for yet another ten."

She refused to give him the key.

Czar Eagle was sad to hear what happened, but they travelled on. They roamed far and wide, over fields and forests, until again they came to a large, beautiful town. Czar Eagle turned to Ivan the merchant's son:

"Go to a certain house in this town and ask the lady of the house for the gold key to the cellar."

Ivan went to the certain house and asked the lady for the gold key to her cellar. She became thoughtful, then said, "It must be my brother Czar Eagle who sends you here. I have not seen him for ten years now, and I don't need to see him for yet another ten."

She refused to give him the key.

Czar Eagle was grieved to hear what happened, but they travelled on. They went far and wide, over fields and forests, until they stopped once again by a large, beautiful town. Czar Eagle turned to Ivan the merchant's son, "Go to a certain house in this town and ask the lady of the house for the gold key to her cellar."

Ivan the merchant's son went to the certain house and asked the lady for the gold key to the cellar.

She was a beautiful maiden, who was delighted at his words and said, "It must be my brother Czar Eagle who sends you here. I have not seen him for ten years, and I have missed him so, I can hardly wait to see him again! He can do what he likes with all the treasures in the cellar."

Then she gave Ivan the gold key.

Czar Eagle was thrilled with all this and went to visit this youngest sister of his with

Ivan. They relaxed, bathed, and ate their fill and after that the Czar married his sister to the merchant's son. Then he bade them both goodbye and went on alone.

Czar Eagle travelled on and on, over fields, over mountains, until he came to a large, imposing town. An evil sorcerer named Immortal Wizzy ruled there. The beautiful daughter of a merchant was imprisoned in his palace. When Czar Eagle heard this, he thought, "My sister has Ivan for a husband, and now I will wed Kate, the daughter of a merchant."

He changed into locksmith's clothes and went to the palace. As Immortal Wizzy was absent, he was allowed in.

For a while Czar Eagle lived in the palace, mending locks and filing keys, until at last he came to Kate, the merchant's daughter. He wasted no time in telling her he had come to set her free and to marry her.

Beautiful Kate threw her arms round his neck and cried, "Alas, Czar Eagle, you must return home, for no one can help me. Immortal Wizzy will return any moment and both you and I will be doomed."

Czar Eagle would not listen, but tried to cheer Kate up. They stayed together three days and three nights, wondering how to escape from the black palace and the powerful Immortal Wizzy.

Then the wizard came back as suddenly as lightning, stormed at Kate, choked Czar Eagle to death, and then flew away again. Poor, beautiful Kate cried and cried till she had no tears left.

Some time later a baby son was born to Kate — the son of Czar Eagle. Kate was so happy, but so worried too. She feared what Immortal Wizzy would do upon his return, wondering if he would harm the child. Because she was so afraid, she put her son into a barrel, with a note saying whose child he was. Then she let the barrel float away on the river which flowed round the palace, hoping that perhaps some kind folk would find it and take care of her son.

That very night Ivan the merchant's son had a dream: he dreamed his ship sailed into the port with a most precious load. He was surprised at such a dream, for he was not expecting the arrival of any of his ships at that time; nevertheless he decided to stroll to the docks and take a look. What did he find there but the barrel with the baby boy! He read the note which told him that this was the son of beautiful Kate, the merchant's daughter, and Czar Eagle, who was choked to death by the wicked wizard Immortal Wizzy. Ivan and his wife shed many tears for the little boy, and took him in as one of their own. They named him Vania, and as they had two other sons, they brought up the three together as brothers.

One day the boys had an argument and the real sons said to Vania, "You're not really one of us! Father found you in a barrel!"

Vania was most upset to learn this and crawled into the loft to have a cry. And there among a pile of rubbish he found the very barrel with the note saying whose child he was. Vania climbed down from the loft and said to his uncle, "I know now that I am not your son, but your nephew. My father is the late Czar Eagle and my mother the beautiful Kate, who is held a prisoner by the wicked wizard Immortal Wizzy. Thank you, uncle, for bringing me up, but now I must leave you, set my mother free and avenge my father."

His cousins, uncle and aunt tried to change his mind, but in vain. Vania stood firm, said goodbye and left.

He went far and wide, over fields and forests, till at last he reached the town where the wicked sorcerer Wizzy reigned and where his mother was held a prisoner. Vania entered the town and walked round the wizard's palace. He was wondering how to get inside. Suddenly he noticed an elderly lady hobble out of the palace gates, a stick in her hand, a sack on her shoulders. She saw Vania and said, "Well I never! So the son has come for his mother! Welcome to you, Vania Eagle!"

"How is it you know me? I have never seen you before," Vania marvelled.

"I know what I know, I see what I see, that is none of your business, young lad. But I will help you if you like. I see your mother every day, for she lets me have the left-overs of food to take home in this sack, so I would not die of hunger."

Vania was glad and begged the old lady to deliver a note to his mother. In this note he wrote:

"Dearest mother, I am your son, whom you once had sent down the river in a barrel. Kind people found me and brought me up, but now I have come to rescue you. Ask Immortal Wizzy where is his Death. He will lie twice, but he will tell you the truth the third time."

"You have thought it out well, Vania Eagle! You have written it well too," the old lady said in approval, as he handed her the letter, though she had not even read it. "Come back here in three days time, and I will give you the answer."

When Vania's mother read the letter, she cried with joy. She knew that her hour of freedom was approaching. When that night Wizzy returned, she was most attentive, making him tea, preparing supper. Afterwards she asked, "Tell me, dear Wizzy, how is it you're immortal? Where is your Death?"

"Why do you want to know?"

"So I could protect you from Death."

"I can look after myself," Wizzy mumbled, but when Vania's mother kept on at him, he said, to keep her quiet, "My death is in the horns of the white cow, which is in my stable."

The next morning Kate had the cow brought into the palace. She garnished its horns with flowers and stood it in the middle of the carpet of their best room.

When Immortal Wizzy returned that evening, he was most surprised.

"What is the meaning of this?" he asked.

"I have placed this cow here, because its horns contain my most precious possession."

Wizzy was quite moved at her words and said, "My death does not lie in the horns of this cow; it lies in the horns of the white goat, which is in my sty."

Kate had the white goat brought to the palace the next morning. She decorated its horns with flowers and placed it on a carpet in their very best room.

When Immortal Wizzy returned that evening he was most surprised to see this.

"What does it mean?" he asked.

"I have put this goat here because in its horns lies my most precious possession," said Kate.

Wizzy was most moved again to see how much she cared and said, "My Death lies not in the horns of that goat. Beyond nine mountains and nine forests stands an oak tree; in this oak is a cupboard and in this cupboard is a duck; the duck holds an egg in its beak and that is where my Death lies."

Vania's mother sat down straight away to write all this in a letter. The following morning she gave it to the old woman, who took it to Vania.

Vania set out on his long journey. He walked on and on, crossing mountains and dales, further and further, till he was weak with hunger. When he saw a mother bear with her young by the path, he thought he would kill one of the babes for food. The mother bear, however, spoke to him in a human voice, "Let my children be! You may stifle your hunger for a while with their flesh, but the pain you would give me would last for ever."

"You are right," said Vania and walked on.

Further away he saw a falcon with little falcons perched on a rock, and he thought of shooting one for food. But the falcon spoke to him in a human voice, "Let my children be! You may stifle your hunger for a while with their flesh, but the pain you would give me would last for ever."

"You are right," agreed Vania and walked on.

On the shores of the sea he saw a fish tossing on the sands and he thought he would kill it and satisfy his hunger. But the fish spoke to him in a human voice, "Throw me back in the water instead. My flesh would not stifle your hunger for ever and you would cause my children pain for the rest of their lives."

"You are right," Vania agreed, tossed the fish in the ocean and walked on.

At last he came to the high oak tree, in which was hidden the cupboard with the duck, which had the egg with Wizzy's Death in its beak.

How could he get at the cupboard? Vania was at his wits end, when suddenly the mother bear appeared, leant with all her strength against the oak and shook it till the little cupboard fell to the ground. It broke as it fell, and the duck flew high into the sky.

How could Vania catch it when it was so high? Suddenly the falcon appeared, pursued the duck and caught it; the duck dropped the egg in its flight and it fell into the sea.

How could he get the egg out of the deep water? Suddenly the fish rose from the waves and floated to the shore. In its mouth it held the egg and passed it to Vania. He took it gladly and happily started on the journey back with the precious egg with Wizzy's Death in his hand.

From that very moment Immortal Wizzy was gravely ill. He lay in his bed, and could hardly move. Day by day he grew steadily worse.

One day he was particularly bad. That was the day when Vania returned with the egg,

walked daringly into the palace and straight to Wizzy's bedroom. As he entered the room, he tripped over the threshold. He fell and squashed the egg. That was the end of Immortal Wizzy.

"What a shame that your poor father, Czar Eagle, did not live to see this," Kate said to her son.

The old lady who helped by taking the letters suddenly came in and said, "Take the broken egg, Vania Eagle, and go with it to the cemetery. Dig out the grave of your father and rub his dead body with this egg."

Vania did as he was bid by the old lady, and lo and behold! His father, Czar Eagle, was suddenly as alive and well as before!

Everyone rejoiced to see Czar Eagle in the palace instead of the wicked wizard. Ivan the merchant's son and Czar Eagle's sister were sent for to help them celebrate. Their sons came too, and they all lived together happily for the rest of their lives. Czar Eagle was a wise ruler, loved by his people, for none of them were ever again poor and no one ever again started a quarrel or a war.

GRANNY
WHO KNEW
EVERYTHING

Once there was a granny and she was such a clever old lady, she had enough brains for everyone. The baron heard about her great wisdom and sent his carriage to fetch her. He had lost a beautiful gold ring with a huge diamond and he hoped granny would be able to find it for him.

Granny did not want to go to the palace, but she had to obey the baron's order. She climbed into the carriage, the coachman cracked his whip and they were off.

In the carriage granny began to pray, "Dear God I know I am a sinner, but leave my punishment till *later* ... yes, *later*. Help me this time please. I'm probably no worse a sinner than the *coachman* ... yes, the *coachman*. Amen."

The coachman out in front heard granny's mutterings, but the only words he seemed to catch properly were *waiter*, *waiter* and then *coachman* and again *coachman*. He was very scared! No wonder too, for it was he and his friend the waiter who stole the gold ring with the huge diamond, from the baron. He stopped the coach, jumped to the ground, and, kneeling before granny, begged her not to give him away. He promised to return the ring and to give her one hundred roubles into the bargain.

"Very well then," agreed granny. "Where did you hide the ring?"

"It hangs on a hook on the ceiling of the stable."

"Leave it there, give me the one hundred roubles and stop worrying!"

When granny reached the palace, the baron welcomed her, saying that tales of her wisdom had come to his ears and that if she found his ring, he would give her one hundred roubles.

Granny nodded her head in agreement and asked the baron to tell her how the ring had disappeared. Then she went to search the palace. After a while she came to the stable, took the ring off the hook and gave it to the baron.

"Here it is, your worship. It is the right one, isn't it?"

"Yes, it is!" cried the baron and asked her where she had found it.

"It found me," granny joked. "The ring rolled behind me." The baron asked no more, but gave granny the promised one hundred roubles. As it was midday, he asked her to stay for lunch.

Granny was restless at the table, whereas the baron made one joke after another. The poor old lady was not used to eating in such a fine way! The baron turned to her and asked whether she could guess what special bird the cook has prepared. The waiter was just bringing in the covered dish.

Granny sighed, "Oh dear, it is not the thing when a village sparrow flies into the dining room of the palace!"

GRANNY WHO KNEW
EVERYTHING

"Excellent," clapped the baron. "This really is a sparrow! How did you guess? You did not even look under the lid."

Granny sighed with relief and wanted nothing else but to get away as quickly as she could. The baron insisted that she must return in his carriage, and asked the coachman to put two dozen eggs under the seat.

But granny did not feel like being driven in style.

"Thank you, kind sir, but no. Riding in style is not for me. I would be as uncomfortable as a hen sitting on eggs. I prefer to go on foot."

The baron never stopped marvelling how this old lady could be so very wise that she knew everything and had all the right answers.

THE CAT AND THE RAM

Once there was an old man and an old woman who lived in a cottage by the edge of the forest. They kept a cat and a ram. One day the old lady put an urn of milk into the cellar, so it would turn to cream. The greedy cat could not resist the temptation and scampered after it.

"Listen, grandfather," said the old lady, "I can hear something rattling below."

"We had better investigate," the old man decided.

When the old lady entered the cellar, she saw that the cat had knocked off the lid and had licked the urn quite clean. She chased the greedy animal out and returned to the kitchen. The cat sneaked in after her and hid behind the stove.

"That wretched cat of ours was in the cellar, grandfather, and it ate all the cream," said the old woman. "You had better drown it!"

When the cat heard this, it ran out of the window to the ram in the pen, and miaowed, "What do you think, ram. The old man and the old woman are going to cut your throat!"

The ram was terrified and the pair made up their minds to run away.

"How can I get out of here when the door of the pen is firmly shut?" worried the ram.

"Leave it to me," said the cat, pushed the handle upwards with its paw, and they were off. They walked on and on, until they found the head of a wolf.

"We will take it with us, it may come in useful," said the cat.

They picked up the wolf's head and went on. Some time later they saw a light in the distance. As they approached, they saw it was a bonfire; twelve wolves sat round it. The cat and the ram were terrified of the wolves, but it was too late to run away. They bravely walked up to the fire. "Good health to you, wolves!" they said.

"And to you too, cat and ram!" the wolves replied.

"What's for supper?" the ram asked the cat after a moment or two.

"What else but one of the twelve wolf heads we have! Go and choose a nice meaty one!" replied the cat.

The ram ran into the bushes and returned with the wolf's head they had found on the way.

"Will this one do, brother cat?"

"Not that one, find a larger one!"

The ram disappeared and reappeared with the very same head.

"What about this one?"

"This one won't do either. Bring the largest, the one which is right at the back!"

The ram went away and returned with the very same head.

"This is the right one," said the cat.

The wolves were most worried when they heard all this.

"How many of our poor brothers must this cat and the ram have killed," they thought and would have liked to take to their heels. But that was impossible. So just four of the wolves stood up and asked the cat and the ram, "Can we go and fetch some wood?"

The cat nodded its head and the wolves ran off. The remaining eight were now really terrified. If the cat and the ram managed twelve wolves between them, what chance had a mere eight? Four more wolves got to their feet, to fetch some water. The cat let them go, "Off with you then, but come back soon!"

After a while the remaining four wolves rose, saying they would go and see why their brothers had not yet returned. The cat allowed them to go, telling them sternly not to waste time but to return speedily with the others.

The twelve wolves raced away.

They ran and ran until they met a bear.

"Where are you running to, grey wolves?" asked the bear.

"To tell the truth, a cat and a ram came to us, bringing with them a pile of wolf heads for their supper! We were afraid we too might be eaten up like our brothers, so we ran away."

"What fools you are," said the bear. "You should have bitten into their throats and eaten them up, instead of running away. Since when have a cat and a ram been eating wolves? Come back with me and we shall see."

"We will all come," they cried.

When the cat and the ram saw the wolves returning with the bear, they were very frightened. The cat ran up a tree, but the ram was not accustomed to climbing, and it got stuck on a low branch.

When the bear and the wolves arrived, they could not see the cat or the ram. The bear said, "Let us sit here under this tree and think where the pair could have got to!"

They sat down and thought.

"Brother cat, brother cat," wailed the ram. "I can't hold on any longer, I'm going to fall!"

"Hold on, hold on! Otherwise we shall be eaten up," whispered the cat.

The ram held on and on, but then the branch snapped and the ram fell down, right on the bear's back.

The cat saw they were in trouble, so quickly it shouted, "Hold it tight now, that bear will do for our breakfast!"

The bear had such a shock, he shook the ram off and ran away as fast as his legs could carry him. The wolves followed right behind him.

By then the cat and the ram had had enough of wandering about. They decided to risk returning to the old man and the old woman in their cottage.

The elderly pair were so pleased to see the ram back, that they forgave the cat for its misdeeds. From that day on the four of them lived happily and in harmony and never fell out again.

POVERTY, DEAR POVERTY

Nobody knows how poverty came into this world, but I will tell you now how it very nearly disappeared from this world for ever. Very, very nearly...

Once there were two brothers. One was rich, the other was as poor as a church mouse. The rich brother lived in town and was a merchant. The poor one lived in an old shack in a village.

One day the poor peasant came to visit his rich brother and begged, "Alas, dear brother! We are so poor, my wife and children have nothing to eat. Please help me!"

"Very well then," agreed the merchant. "But you will have to work for me this week first."

The peasant worked a full week for his brother. He swept the yard, tended the horses, fetched water, chopped wood; he did not stop from morn till night. At the end of the week the merchant gave him three loaves of bread.

"Thank you for the bread," said the poor man and went home.

"Wait a minute," the merchant shouted after him. "It is my birthday next week. We will have a feast, so come and bring your wife!"

When the peasant got home, he gave his wife the three loaves and told her his brother had invited them to celebrate his birthday.

"I am not coming," said the wife. "Many rich guests will be there. What would poor folk like us do among such fine company?"

But the peasant eventually persuaded her to go. Many wealthy merchants were present and there was so much food and wine, the tables were bending under the weight. No one took any notice of the peasant and his wife. No one offered them even a mouthful of food, or a glass of water. When the guests were saying goodbye, they were all merry, singing away. As for the peasant and his wife, their stomachs were rolling with hunger.

"I am going to sing too, even with a rumbling stomach," the peasant said to himself and sang a merry song.

As he was singing, he heard a voice singing with him. He tried again, and heard it once more.

"Who is singing with me?" he wondered.

"It is I, Poverty," said a voice by his side. It belonged to an ugly old hag, as thin as a rake, who grinned at him. The three of them went home together.

The next day Poverty said to the peasant:

"Let us go out to the inn for a drink."

"How can we go to the inn," said the peasant. "I haven't any money and they won't fill our glasses for nothing."

But Poverty would not be put off. "You can sell your sledge. The winter is coming to an end."

So they sold the sledge and drank all the money.

The following day Poverty again said to the peasant, "Come out for a drink."

"I can't," said the peasant. "I haven't anything else to sell."

"You can sell your plough," insisted Poverty. "Spring is still far away."

So they went to the inn and bought drinks with all the money.

The very next day Poverty wanted to go to the inn again. This time the peasant stood firm.

"I am always the one who pays. Now it is your turn. Otherwise I am staying at home."

"All right then," agreed Poverty. "Borrow a horse and a cart from your neighbour."

The peasant borrowed the horse and cart, saying he wanted to get some wood, and set off with Poverty to the forest. When they reached a woodland clearing, Poverty said, "Dig out this tree stump!"

The peasant dug it out and what do you think he found? A heap of gold coins! He loaded them on the cart, which was soon full.

"Now we have plenty of money to take to the inn," laughed Poverty.

The peasant, however, was no fool. What good would the money be if Poverty spent it so fast? thought he. So he said, "Wait a minute. I can see a few more coins right at the bottom. It would be a shame to leave them. You're thinner than I am, climb in and get them!"

Poverty climbed into the hole, and the peasant swiftly rolled the tree stump back in its place—and there she stayed!

Then he returned, built a new house, bought fields, horses, and cows. In a matter of weeks he was the richest farmer in the village. As it happened to be his birthday, he organized a great feast and invited his brother merchant from town to attend.

The brother was surprised to see how his brother had become so rich. The latter smiled and laughed, "Poverty, dear Poverty, helped me to this."

"I can't see how anyone can get rich from poverty," wondered the merchant.

"Poverty showed me where treasure was hidden. If you go to a certain place, you too will find Poverty. I am sure she still sits under the dug-out tree stump on the woodland clearing."

The merchant wasted no time and the very next day went to the forest, rolled the tree stump away and found Poverty, who immediately jumped on his back.

"What an ungrateful rascal you are! I helped you to find treasure and you left me under this stump. Now I'll never leave you!"

The merchant tried vainly to explain that she was mistaking him for his brother. He could not get rid of Poverty. Each day he had to take her to the inn, and his money was soon disappearing in drink. The merchant saw that before long he would be turned into a beggar. "I can't go on like this," he said one day to his wife. "If I don't shake off Poverty soon, we will be penniless."

"Don't you worry," his wife consoled him. "When Poverty asks to be taken to the inn again, tell her that first you would like to play a game of hide-and-seek. Leave the rest to me."

The merchant followed his wife's advice. Poverty did not feel like playing hide-and-seek, but eventually she agreed. The merchant was the first to hide, but Poverty found him straight away. Then Poverty hid, and the merchant could not find her. But his wife had been watching Poverty and saw her climb into an empty bottle, which stood on the stable window. Swiftly the wife ran to the bottle, pushed the cork in firmly and threw the bottle into the river. Let that Poverty drown!

From that day the merchant again prospered.

Poverty, dear Poverty, did not drown, but found yet another poor soul to torment. And she is with us in this world to this day.

THE FOX
AND THE CRANE

The waters of the river Smorodina flow through a dense forest. There, on the shore of the river, lived a fox and also a crane.

One day the fox came to the crane and said, "Do you know what I have read in my books of knowledge?"

"I most certainly do not," answered the crane.

"I read that you and I are cousins."

"That seems very strange to me," said the surprised crane.

"Maybe," agreed the fox. "But if we are related, we should live together in harmony and friendship and should visit each other sometimes."

"Very well, then," said the crane. "Ask me to lunch!"

The fox asked the crane to lunch. He cooked semolina pudding, put it on a plate and when the crane arrived, the fox said, "Please eat as much as you want Crane. It is a good pudding, all milk and honey. You'll enjoy it!"

The crane pecked and pecked with its long beak, but could not get any pudding off the plate. The artful fox ate all the pudding and licked the plate clean.

Some time later it was the crane's turn to invite the fox to dinner. Fish soup was served from a tall jug with a narrow spout. The crane urged the fox, "Eat up, foxie, eat up! It is an excellent soup, all trout and carp. I am sure you've never eaten one like it."

The fox walked round and round the jug, pushing it with its nose and poking its tongue inside, but could not reach the soup. The crane, however, with its long beak soon drank all the soup. Not a single drop was left.

The crane had the last laugh of all!

(102) 103   THE FOX
             AND THE CRANE

THE SOLDIER WHO SERVED
IN HEAVEN AND HELL

In the old days things were different from today. The whole world was different and soldiers had to stay in the army for twenty-five years.

When a certain soldier was released from the army after his twenty-five years service, the sergeant said to him, "As you have served your Czar faithfully for twenty-five years, here are twenty-five coppers and an old patrol bag."

"Good," thought the soldier. "I can buy tobacco with the coppers and I may find some use for the old bag. I'll strap it to my shoulder."

Then he set out on his way home.

It was a long journey, but he managed to survive. Good folk gave him food and drink, and sometimes shelter for the night on the hay or the couch. As the weather was fine, he often slept in the meadow on the soft green grass. So the time passed happily enough.

One night a farmer took him in for the night. As this was a very inquisitive man, as soon as the soldier fell asleep, he examined all his belongings. The soldier really had nothing except the old patrol bag on a strap. When the farmer opened it, a tiny devil jumped out. It was all hairy, with eyes like burning cinders, and he spat, "Why don't you let me sleep?"

The farmer was most frightened. Quickly he closed the bag and shook with fear the rest of the night. The next morning he asked the soldier, "Tell me, what have you inside your patrol bag?"

"Nothing at all," answered the soldier.

"I think the devil's got into it."

"Don't be so silly," laughed the soldier, thinking the farmer must be a little bit mad. He set off again.

Eventually curiosity got the better of him.

"I've had this patrol bag several weeks now and never even opened it," he thought. "Perhaps something really is inside!"

The soldier opened the bag and the hairy imp leapt out again, "What is your wish, soldier?" he asked.

The soldier was startled, but pretended not to be surprised. He said, "Bring me something nice to eat!"

As soon as this was said, the imp disappeared. He flew like an arrow to the village, right through the window of a big farm. From the oven he took a freshly roasted cockerel, from the cellar a bottle of wine. Then he appeared again. The soldier ate and drank, and the little devil asked once more, "Is there anything else you desire, soldier?"

"Yes, there is. I should like to know how you got into my patrol bag."

"I have been put into it by a magic spell. Whoever wears that bag will be my master

THE SOLDIER WHO SERVED
IN HEAVEN AND HELL

for ten years. I must serve him, fulfil his every wish, but at the end of that time I will take him to Hell.''

"So that's how things are." The soldier now understood.

As he was not exactly eager to go to Hell, he wondered how he could avoid it. The imp prattled on, "Anything else you desire, soldier?"

The soldier then had an idea. "Yes. Take me to Heaven right now!" he ordered.

"To Heaven?" The devil seemed afraid.

Then he began to make excuses, trying to make the soldier change his mind.

The soldier stopped him. "You've just said you have to fulfil my every wish, so off we go to Heaven!"

The poor devil could do nothing else. He shrugged his shoulders and sighed and took the soldier to the gates of Heaven. He even knocked on the gates, but of course he could not go inside. He sat on a cloud and wondered what could happen.

Nothing extraordinary did happen. Saint Peter allowed the soldier inside and the soldier breathed a sigh of relief that it had all ended so happily.

Heaven really was a lovely place. There were beautiful scented flowers everywhere, birds singing happily, and angels playing their harps. But somehow the soldier felt rather out of place. What good was all this to a simple soldier? They had no tobacco, there was not a single inn to go to for a drink or a game of cards. They really should have had an inn.

The soldier went to Saint Peter and said, "Look, Saint Peter, I think your Heaven is very nice, but it is not the right place for a soldier. What would you say if I opened an inn up here?"

Saint Peter stroked his long beard, scratched behind his ear and said he wasn't exactly against the idea, but he would have to ask God first. So they both went to see God.

Their master was most angry with the soldier for suggesting such a wicked thing. Before he knew what was happening, the soldier found himself thrown out of the Heaven gates, and as the devil was still sitting there, he caught him by the sleeve and said, "And now, dear soldier, I'll take you to Hell. You'll get there one day anyway, so why wait?"

"That's true," agreed the soldier. "They wouldn't let me back into Heaven, so I might as well try it in Hell. Perhaps it won't be quite so dull."

Hell was certainly far from dull. There was plenty of drinking and singing; the souls of sinners played cards with devils all day long and there was as much tobacco as anyone could smoke. The soldier was in his element and he said smugly:

"If I had realized what fun it is in Hell, I would have come right from my birth."

After a month or two the soldier began to pine for the world. He started to miss a lot of things; the sun never shone in Hell, the grass never grew, there was not a bird to be heard, not a breath of wind to be felt. The soldier pined more and more, till he felt he could not bear to stay a moment longer. He wondered how he could get out of Hell and back on Earth again. He thought and thought, until he remembered how it all ended in Heaven. Then he smiled happily.

An old pope, who became the soldier's friend in Hell, was playing cards with the soldier one day, when the soldier said:

"Listen, old chap, what if we opened a church in here? You could be the pope and I would be your church warden."

"That's not a bad idea," said the old man. "In fact it's quite a splendid idea. But we'll have to ask Lucifer first."

They went to see Lucifer.

Lucifer was absolutely furious, how dared they suggest such a thing. A church in Hell! As it seemed obvious they could not appreciate Hell, Lucifer made them both pack their belongings and as a punishment sent them both to Heaven. When they knocked on the heavenly gates, Saint Peter answered. He let the pope in with no hesitation at all, but shut the gates in the soldier's face. He remembered him all too well!

The soldier stood before the gates; he was not allowed to enter Heaven and he had been thrown out of Hell. What now?

He opened his old patrol bag which he still possessed. The imp jumped out and the soldier said to him, "Now, my friend, please take me back to Earth!"

As soon as he had spoken, he flew like the wind, until he had to close his eyes. When he opened them again, he found himself in a forest clearing. The sun was shining, the birds were singing, and the scent of the wood was so wonderful that the soldier could not breathe in enough of it. He rubbed his eyes and said, "I am not really sure if I dreamt it all, or if I have actually been to Heaven and Hell. But whatever happened, I am sure now that the best place is here on Earth."

Then he rose and set off on his journey home. But first he took the old patrol bag from his shoulder and tossed it as far away as he could down the gorge.

THE PAUPER WHO ONLY HAD
A COW AND AN OLD GOAT

In a certain village there once lived a poor peasant. Foma was his name. This pauper had a crumbling old shack to sleep in. He did not own a field. In fact, all he owned was a cow and an old goat. The cow, unfortunately, ate some poisonous weed, swelled up and was dead by morning.

The pauper was terribly upset. "I really have a terrible life!" he complained. Heavy hearted, he skinned the poor old cow and took the hide to sell to a tanner in town.

On his way there he passed a lonely building. It was a very nice farm. The pauper glanced into the kitchen and saw the farmer's wife and another dozen females sitting round the table, feasting as if they were in the palace! They had delicious fat geese, bottles of vodka — all one could wish for. Foma was extremely hungry, so he knocked on the window. But the farmer's wife chased him off. "Mind your own business and go and find somewhere else to sleep. There is no place for you here!"

As soon as she had spoken, they heard the rattle of a carriage. The farmer's wife grew pale. "Oh dear, what a calamity!" she cried. "The farmer is returning from town. I thought he would stay overnight and he's back already. I shall be in trouble for having this party."

Pauper Foma started to console her. "Don't let it bother you, ma'am. Give me fifty roubles and I will put everything right."

He began giving orders to put the geese into the oven, the vodka into the pantry, the visitors into the loft.

The minute everything and everyone was put away, the farmer came through the gates and asked what was going on. Foma explained that he was asking the farmer's wife to give him bed and food, but she did not want to let him in during her husband's absence.

"She is quite right too," agreed the farmer with satisfaction. "But as I am back now, you might as well come in. You can sleep over the stove."

Foma entered, with the hide across his shoulder.

"What have you got there?" asked the farmer. "It is from a cow, isn't it?"

"You're quite wrong," laughed Foma. "This is Magician Spotty."

"Magician Spotty?" The farmer shook his head in disbelief. "What sort of magic does he do?"

"All sorts."

"Let him conjure up something nice to eat then," suggested the farmer laughingly. "I am as hungry as a wolf."

"That will be easy," said Foma. Taking the hide by the tail, he pressed it to his ear, pretending to listen. Then he turned to the farmer. "Magician Spotty has conjured up something delicious in the oven," he said.

THE PAUPER WHO ONLY HAD
A COW AND AN OLD GOAT

"We'll see," said the farmer and to his amazement pulled out a stream of geese from the oven.

He sat down to feast and Foma did not wait to be asked twice.

"This really is very good," said the farmer, smacking his lips. "Do you think that magician of yours could also conjure up a bottle or two of something to warm our blood?"

Pauper Foma once again placed the hide's tail by his ear and told the farmer he would find vodka in the pantry.

"Well, well," muttered the farmer in wonder, as he brought the vodka into the kitchen.

When they had eaten and drunk, the farmer remarked, "Now let this magician of yours tell me what is in my house that I don't know about."

Once again Foma placed the cow's tail to his ear and said, "Up there in the loft is a whole nest of witches."

"I beg your pardon?" the farmer stuttered with fear.

"It is true, come on, let's take a look."

The farmer was really afraid to go, so Foma of course suggested he waited in the hall, saying that he would go up alone and chase them out.

The females were huddled by the chimney breast, waiting to see what would happen.

"Everything is fine," Foma assured them. "All you have to do now is to run out of here as you are able. But you mustn't look round, no matter what is going on."

While he was talking, Foma put his hands inside the chimney and blackened all their faces with soot.

The waiting farmer saw the gang of females rush down the stairs — hair sticking on end, faces black, gleaming eyes—and his teeth chattered just from the sight! They flew past him like the wind.

"Good riddance," spat the farmer. "You really must sell me that magician."

"No fear," said the pauper. "You can have these pieces for fifty roubles, but you can't have the magician."

The farmer counted out fifty roubles, but afterwards kept pleading with Foma, till the latter agreed to sell the whole hide for two hundred roubles.

"First Magician Spotty has to get used to you," said Foma to the farmer. "Before you try him out, you must sleep on him two nights running."

The farmer went to sleep on the cow's hide, while Foma slept over the stove. Next morning he set off home merrily. He bought vodka, gherkins, fresh bread and ham. He sat on his doorstep and ate with relish. A magistrate came by and said, "What's this, what's this? Yesterday your cow dropped dead and today you're behaving as if you had inherited a farm."

"I did not inherit a farm," said Foma. "But I sold the hide from my cow for three hundred roubles."

"Three hundred roubles?" wondered the magistrate. "You could very nearly buy a whole herd for such a sum."

"Perhaps hide has gone up in price," Foma said, pulling a face. He took a swig from the bottle of vodka and emptied a pile of gold roubles from his pocket.

"Who gave you so much money for the skin?" asked the magistrate.

"The farmer who lives on the lonely farm on the way to town," explained Foma.

The magistrate said nothing, but went home. The same night he slaughtered his ten cows, skinned them and hurried to the farmer.

The next day he was back. He flew into Foma's kitchen furious with rage. He told him how the farmer had thrown him out, skins and all; how he had set his hounds on him and called him a swindler and an insolent thief.

"Well, that isn't my fault," the pauper defended himself. "So the farmer gave me three hundred roubles, and gave you a hiding. That is his business, not mine. Now I must go and squeeze my goat."

"Squeeze your goat?" wondered the magistrate and followed Foma curiously.

The pauper went into the pen, and pulled the goat outside. Secretly he placed a gold rouble into its mouth. Then he gave it a sharp blow with a stick. The goat bucked, bleated and spat out the gold coin. The pauper picked it up, put it into his pocket and led the goat back into the pen.

"These are strange happenings," muttered the magistrate. "Does this goat spit out gold roubles every day?"

"Yes, every day. I am waiting to see how long it will last."

"Sell me that goat," said the magistrate. "It will make up for what I've lost over my cows."

The pauper did not want to sell, but in the end he agreed. He sold the goat very cheaply, for ten roubles, in fact.

At noon the next day the magistrate was back again, shouting and raving that the goat had stopped spitting out gold coins.

"I did tell you I had no idea how long it would last," said Foma, but refused to take the goat back. The pauper did suggest, however, he would strike another bargain with the magistrate.

"I am not likely to listen to you again," said the furious officer. "You've cheated me twice, but it won't happen a third time!"

Then he gave instructions to his people to catch Foma, tie him up in a sack and drown him in the river. When they had dragged the poor chap as far as the shore, Foma started to cry, "Good Christians, go first at least to say a prayer for me in the church. Pray that my soul may be saved before you drown me."

"Yes, we should say a prayer first," agreed the magistrate. They left Foma in his sack by the river and went to church. He wailed and wailed, as if someone was sticking knives into him.

A shepherd who was taking his herd of cows past the spot, wondered who was making such a pathetic noise.

"Of course I am crying," sobbed Foma. "Who wouldn't cry in my place! They want to make me into a magistrate, but I don't want to be one. So they put me in this sack, to make sure I won't run away."

"What a stupid fellow you are," said the astonished shepherd. "I'd love to be a magistrate!"

"In that case crawl into this sack instead of me!"

Before the men returned from church, the shepherd was tied in the sack and Foma and the herd were hidden in the bushes.

The men tossed the sack into the river and it floated away swiftly with the current; goodness knows where the shepherd ended up! When everyone had gone, Foma drove the cattle out of the bushes and straight into the village. The astonished magistrate couldn't utter a single word!

"I'll tell you what happened," the pauper said in explanation. "When you threw me into the river, the sack tore and I suddenly found myself in an enormous meadow where there were masses of cows. I drove these few to the shore, but you should see how many were left!"

The magistrate still said nothing, but ran to the river and jumped right in. Maybe he is still looking for cows somewhere far away, wherever the current has taken him.

THE WOODEN EAGLE

On a doorstep of a certain inn in Moscow sat three fellows drinking heavily. One of them said, "If only I had some money, you'd see what I would do!"

"What would you do?"

"I'd go to the market, buy a lot of metal and make a whole regiment of metal soldiers. They would win every war."

"That's nothing," swaggered the second fellow. "If I had the money, I'd go to the market to buy some gold; then I would make a gold drake which would swim in water, fly in the air and peck only gold corn."

"Even that's nothing," said the third. "I would buy some wood and carve a wooden eagle which could circle the world in just one week."

It so happened that the Czar's clerk was sitting in the inn, listening to all that was said. He hastened to the Czar and told him that in a certain inn three fellows were drinking, who could make unheard of things from metal, gold and wood. The Czar straight away asked to see them.

When they came to the Czar he said, "I welcome you, young men!"

"Good health to you, Your Majesty the Czar!"

"I was told you could make unheard of things from metal, gold and wood. Is this true?"

"It is true."

"What can you do then?" the Czar asked the first fellow.

"I can make a wholle regiment of soldiers out of metal, who would win all wars."

"And you?"

"I can make a drake from a lump of gold, which could swim in water, fly in the air and peck only gold corn."

"What about you?"

"I can carve a wooden eagle which would circle the world in just one week."

"Get on with it then," said the Czar. "Bring your work to me in a month's time," and he gave each of them a bag of gold coins.

The three fellows returned to the inn to drink to their good fortune. The first two soon left to go home, but the third remained in the inn the whole month, until all his money was spent.

"There's nothing else for it," he said to himself, "but to get on with the job. I must deliver the wooden eagle to the Czar tomorrow." He wiped his chin and went home to work.

He found some pieces of wood and some nails in his shed, then he made some glue. All through the night he sawed and carved, rubbed down and polished. When the morning sun came out, he was already finished. He put the wooden eagle on his back and went to

the Czar's palace. His friends the blacksmith and the goldsmith were standing in the yard, waiting for the Czar to wake up.

At last the Czar appeared and said, "Nice to see you all! Show me now what you have made."

The blacksmith cried, "Attention!" And a whole regiment of metal soldiers stood before them; such soldiers who would win any war.

"Well done," said the Czar and gave the blacksmith a bag of gold and sent him home. The soldiers he sent to his general.

It was the goldsmith's turn next. Proudly he pulled out a gold drake and put it in the fountain which was in the yard. The drake swam about merrily, then flew about in the air and pecked gold corn.

"Excellent," said the Czar. He gave the goldsmith a bag of gold coins and sent him home. The drake was given to his servant for safe keeping.

Then it was the carpenter's turn to demonstrate his wooden eagle. He placed it on the ground, and sat astride its back. The eagle flapped its wings and flew away. Exactly a week later it returned, after circling the whole world. The Czar was so impressed he gave the carpenter two bags of gold, and took the wooden eagle into his own chamber.

The Czar had a young son and as this boy was most inquisitive of course he found the wooden eagle in his father's room. He jumped onto its back and suddenly the eagle rose and flew through the open window far, far away.

The Czar's son flew one day, two days, then the third. At last, by nightfall, the eagle came down in the middle of a dense forest.

The young man hid the eagle in some bushes, then went on alone. After a while he came to a clearing, where a small cottage stood. He entered and found a grey old man sitting by the stove.

"Good evening, grandfather!" he said in greeting.

But the old man remained silent.

The Czar's son then spoke in German, but the old man still did not answer. The youth tried English, but that too was no good. Only when he spoke in French did the old man reply and asked immediately:

"Where are you from, young man?"

"I am the son of a merchant from Moscow, grandfather. I was sailing the seas with my father on business, when there was a big storm. Our boat sank and I alone escaped with my life."

The old man was sorry for the youth, so he gave him food and drink and a bed for the night. The following day he sent him to Paris.

As soon as the Czar's son reached Paris, he went to the very best inn. He sat down and ordered food and drink, though his pockets were completely empty.

The waiters were surprised to see this young man dressed so strangely. They told the landlord about him and he came to the table and asked questions. The young man said, "I am the son of a Moscow merchant. We were sailing the seas on business, when a great storm wrecked our boat. I alone escaped with my life."

The landlord suggested, "I have no son of my own. Stay here and be my son."

So the youth stayed.

After a few weeks he asked the landlord, "Please father, buy me an organ with twelve notes. I will play it, and the clients will like it."

The landlord bought the organ with the twelve notes. His new son played each evening and their clients enjoyed the music so much that all of them started coming only to this particular inn and nowhere else. Landlords of all the other inns became penniless.

They grew very angry and went to complain to the French King himself. "Your Royal Highness, we have come to complain about the landlord of the best inn in Paris. He now employs some foreign youth who plays the organ with twelve notes so beautifully that all the clients love it. In fact they only go to that certain inn; not a single soul strays our way, so now we are penniless."

The King was most displeased to hear this, so he drove in his carriage to the very best inn in town. He stormed at the landlord, "I have a complaint about you! They say all the customers come to your inn and the others are left empty. I believe you have a youth here who plays the organ with the twelve notes most beautifully. It is because of him everyone comes here and nowhere else."

"This is true," agreed the landlord and called the youth.

"Who are you and where are you from?" asked the King.

"I am the son of a merchant from Moscow. My father and I were sailing the seas on business. Then a storm overtook us, wrecked our boat and I alone escaped with my life."

The King then said, "I have no son, only a disobedient daughter. Stay with me and be my son!"

After the Czar's son had lived in the royal palace for two weeks, the King took him aside and asked him to look out of the window.

"Tell me, my son, what do you see?" he asked.

"I see a white tower."

"That tower lies fifteen miles from Paris. My disobedient daughter is locked up in it. I wanted her to marry the English King, but she did not do as she was told. She actually ran away from the altar! Now she must sit in the tower and not see any man at all. If she disobeys, not only my daughter, but also the man will lose his head!"

The Czar's son asked the servants about the disobedient princess, but nobody wanted even to talk about her. He did learn, however, that the princess was extremely beautiful, but that no one could get near her, for she was well guarded at the entrance to the tower.

The Czar's son decided he would set the princess free. He went to the dense forest, where he had left the wooden eagle hidden in the thicket. When it grew dark, he sat astride the bird and flew straight to the tower where the disobedient princess was held a prisoner. The eagle came to her very window. The youth knocked on it gently.

"Who is it?" asked the princess.

"It is I, the son of the Czar of Moscow. I have come to rescue you."

The princess was naturally terribly thrilled to hear this. She opened the window to let him in, fed him with cakes, sweets and wine and then said, "Dear friend, I cannot run away with you just now, because I am not very well. Travelling through the air would do me harm, in fact it could bring on my death. Wait for another seven days. On the seventh I shall be well again and will fly off with you."

The Czar's son agreed and promised to visit the princess each night on his wooden eagle, until she grew better. This he did.

A certain alert guard in this tower noticed that some strange huge bird flew to the princess's window each night, and did not fly away again till just before dawn. He reported this to the King. The King immediately hastened to his daughter and demanded to know who flew to her each night. But the princess answered, "I certainly know nothing about someone flying to my window in the night, dear father. Plenty of night birds and bats circle round the tower, but nobody enters my room."

The King did not believe his daughter and told the servants to paint the window with glue. Then the big bird would be caught.

The following morning the King returned at dawn to examine the window, but the glue was no longer there. As it happened, as the Czar's son let himself in through the window, it rubbed off onto his trousers. The King said nothing, but returned to the palace and there he met the Czar's son. The youth was whistling merrily. The King looked down at his trousers and saw they were smeared with glue.

"Where did you get your trousers so dirty?" he asked sternly.

"I honestly don't know, dear father."

"But I do!" stormed the King, and straight away gave the order for the youth to be tied up, and his daughter too. Then they were both led to the scaffold.

Now the Czar's son and the princess were in real trouble. Already they were by the gallows, already the hangman was holding the noose. The Czar's son suddenly spoke up:

"Listen, dear father! Surely everyone who is sentenced to death can make a last request. Is not this true?"

"That is true," agreed the King.

"In that case let me have my last request!"

"Very well. What is your wish?"

"In the bushes of the dense forest you will find a wooden eagle. I used to fly on it to my dearest princess. Before I die, I should like to sit on it for the last time to say goodbye."

The King agreed and sent his servants to the forest to find the wooden eagle and bring it to the Czar's son. When this was done, the Czar's son sat on its back, snatched the princess and sat her behind him. Before anyone knew what was happening, they were high in the clouds.

The King immediately ordered the soldiers to aim the most powerful cannon at them, the largest they had in France, and to shoot them down to the ground. But by the time the cannon was brought, by the time the cannon was loaded, by the time they took aim and fired, the Czar's son and his princess were far, far away. In fact they were already over his native Moscow, right above the palace. The wooden eagle gently came down into the palace gardens.

The Czar of Moscow was so happy to see his son return with the wooden eagle and with such a beautiful and noble bride. A huge wedding was soon prepared and all Moscow was asked to attend.

The three friends who started all this came too: the blacksmith, the goldsmith and the carpenter. They drank and they danced, they ate and they sang. But they did not brag about what they would do if only they had the money. They preferred just to drink, and drink, and drink, and drink, and perhaps they are still there drinking.

THE MISERLY FARMER
AND THE CLEVER LABOURER

Once there was a farmer who was such a miser that he even counted the peas as his wife was putting them in the pot. This farmer employed a farmhand called Vania and he had more brains in his little finger than his master had in his head!

One evening the farmer said to the labourer, "Vania, tomorow morning we shall go and gather the corn."

"Very well then," agreed Vania.

The next morning they rose early and the farmer said:

"Give us our breakfast, woman!"

The farmer's wife put breakfast before them; they ate it, wiped their beards on their sleeve, then the farmer pondered, "It would be a waste of time to come back home at noon for lunch. It would be better to eat right now. Wife, bring us our dinner!"

The wife gave them lunch; they ate till they were fit enough to burst.

"It would be silly for her to have to bring tea to us! We might as well have our tea now," the farmer decided and was pleased to see he would save some money, for Vania could not eat it all. In fact he had only a cup of milk and left all else.

The farmer then said:

"When we return from the field at night, we'll be too tired to enjoy our food. Wife, you might as well bring us our supper right now!"

The wife brought supper, but Vania could not even look at more food. The farmer laughed and laughed.

"Come on, let's tackle that corn now!"

Vania replied, "No fear, master! After supper one goes to bed. So good night!"

And he went to the loft to sleep, leaving behind an infuriated farmer.

IVAN AND PRINCESS
BLUE-EYES

In a certain Czardom, in a kingdom — but not in the one we are living in — there once ruled Czar Bel Belanin. He had three sons: Vasilij, Fjodor and Ivan. For thirty years Czar Bel Belanin sat in his palace. He did not saddle his horse, he did not even take a sword in his hand. Then suddenly he decided to ride out and meet other people. He rode all day long, until the red sky marked the approach of the night. Just then he came across fresh footprints, so deep that his horse fell into them up to its knees. The Czar was puzzled. "I wonder who rode through here?"

He journeyed on till he saw a white tent with a horse by its side. In the tent was Princess Blue-eyes.

"Who are you and what do you want here?" she asked.

"I went for a ride, to see new places and fresh faces. Surely there is nothing wrong in that?" he replied.

"Maybe yes and maybe no. In any case I challenge you. We will ride against each other from a distance of a horse's three steps and a horse's three jumps. Then we shall see."

They rode against each other from a distance of three leaps and three steps, raising their metal clubs, long lances and sharp swords. They charged and clashed with such violence that sparks were flying, but they both remained seated in their saddles. They charged again and met again and again both stayed in their saddles. When they charged the third time, the Czar's horse tripped and threw his master from the saddle. Princess Blue-eyes jumped to the ground, and, kneeling across the Czar's chest, she wrenched both his eyes out and hid them behind her right cheek. Then she sat the Czar back on his horse, smacked its hide and said, "Take this poor human flesh home!"

When Czar Bel Belanin came home, his eldest sons were looking out for him from their window. They went to meet him. "Welcome home, father! You left in good health, we hope you stayed in good health and returned in good health."

Then the sons noticed that their father's eyes were gone and he told them what Princess Blue-eyes did to him.

Fjodor and Vasilij then chose the best horses, the longest lances and the sharpest swords, and rode after the wicked princess. For three years after no one saw them again.

It was then that the youngest son, Ivan, came to his father to tell him he would go to look for his brothers and the princess.

At first the Czar would not hear of it, but when his son insisted, he let him go after all.

Ivan took a sharp sword and a very long lance, but he did not like any of the horses, so he set off on foot. He walked and walked till he reached a cross-road. There was a signpost by the side, which read:

"Take the left turn, and you will marry. Take the right turn, and you will eat, drink and be merry. Go straight on and you will lose your head, so do not tarry."

Ivan thought a moment about the sign. He certainly did not wish to lose his head, and as he was neither hungry nor thirsty, he took the left turn. He walked on and on till he came to a tiny cottage. A beautiful maiden greeted him on the doorstep:

"Welcome, Ivan! I have waited for you for three years, three months and three days. Come in, sit at the oak table; I will feed you with vegetables and fish, quench your thirst with green wine and make you rest in a soft white bed."

Ivan sat at the table with the lovely maiden. They ate the fish and vegetables, downing it with the green wine.

"Now lay down in the soft white bed, Ivan!"

But Ivan seized the beautiful maiden, pushed her into the bed and the bed turned upside down, throwing the maiden into a black cellar.

"Who is down there?" cried Ivan.

"It is I, Fjodor."

Ivan let his very long lance down into the cellar and pulled his brother up. Poor Fjodor was covered in wounds, and was as black as soot and overgrown with moss.

"Ivan, please pull me out too!" cried the beautiful maiden from below.

"No I won't. You will go black too, and overgrown with moss. Then you'll lose all your beauty."

"Please pull me out, Ivan! I will give you a heroic horse, faster than any other in the world. There is only one other horse which is faster — and that is its brother."

Ivan decided such a heroic horse would be most useful, so he pulled the beautiful maiden out of the black cellar. She led him to the stables and gave him the heroic horse. It was full of high spirits, waiting for its new master. Ivan jumped into the saddle, sat his brother behind him, and off they rode back to the cross-road.

As they were hungry and thirsty, they took the right turn. They rode on and on, until they reached a small cottage. An ugly old hag was waiting for them on the doorstep. "Welcome, Ivan! I have been waiting for you for three years, three months and three days. Come in, sit yourself down in the cedar armchair by the oak table and we shall have a meal of fish and vegetables and drink green wine.

But Ivan seized the ugly old hag, threw her into the armchair, and it turned upside down, throwing the ugly old hag into a dark cellar.

"Who is down there?" Ivan cried.

"It is I, Vasilij."

Ivan took his extra long lance, lowered it into the cellar and pulled his brother out. Poor Vasilij was covered in wounds, and was as black as soot, and overgrown with moss.

"Please, Ivan, pull me out too!" begged the old woman from below.

"No I won't! You too will go as black as soot and overgrown with moss, and you'll be even uglier than you are now!"

"Ivan, please pull me out! I will give you a bottle of water, but it will not be ordinary water. It will be dead water, which will heal any wound, but will kill the person. And I will give you another bottle, but it will also contain no ordinary water. This is the water of life, which does not heal wounds, but brings all corpses back to life so that they are healthier and more handsome than ever before."

Ivan was delighted to hear he would have the water of death and the water of life, and pulled the ugly hag out of the cellar. As soon as she gave him the two bottles, Ivan tried them out. When he sprinkled both his brothers with the dead water, their wounds healed, but they stopped breathing. When he sprinkled them with the life water, they rose before him, no longer blackened and overgrown with moss, but healthier and more handsome than they had ever been. Ivan jumped into his saddle, sat his brothers behind him and they rode back to the cross-road. There he said to them:

"Return to our father, dear brothers, to Czar Bel Belanin. I will ride on alone."

The brothers thanked Ivan and bade him goodbye, then turned towards home. Ivan now took the middle road. He rode on and on, for a while and for a long time, near and far, high and low, higher than the deep forests, lower than the high clouds. Suddenly he came upon a cottage built on a wooden pillar.

"Little shack, little shack, turn to me with your back!"

The cottage turned with the door towards him and Ivan went inside. Old woman Jaga sat by the stove; all skin and bones. In one corner there was one of her legs, in another corner the second leg; in the other corners were her arms. The head was in the cellar, filthy with grime; her metal nose stuck out of the chimney.

"What brought you here?" she asked.

"You're a fine one! You haven't yet given me anything to eat or drink, and already you are asking questions."

Old woman Jaga gave Ivan food and drink, then said, "Did you come willingly or unwillingly?"

"I came because it is my duty to do so," answered Ivan and told her everything. Then he asked if she knew the way to Princess Blue-eyes.

"I know the princess well; she does not live far, only a mere twenty thousand miles away. Go to sleep now, we'll think of something by morning."

When Ivan woke the next day, he said to the woman, "Granny Jaga, sit your clever head on my wide shoulder and lead me to the princess, so that I can take the eyes of my father, Bel Belanin, back to him."

"I have lived here a thousand years now, and many youths have ridden by, but none of them were as wise as you are. Don't worry, I will help you. I will disguise you in my cloak and give you my babbling tom-cat. When you come to the white-stoned Czar's palace, you will enter through iron gates. You will tie your horse to a silver pillar and sit my babbling tom-cat on the pillar; up there it will sing a song, then it will climb down and will tell a story. Its piercing voice will be heard for seven miles and will make everyone's hair stand on end.

You go straight through the gold doors into the palace. Bow to the guards, but do not utter a single word, so they do not realize it is not I. You will find Princess Blue-eyes asleep in the palace. Take your father's eyes from behind her right cheek, but don't do anything else and don't touch anything — just hurry back!"

Ivan thanked Granny Jaga and followed her advice. He jumped astride his heroic horse and was off.

They rode on and on and on, for a while and for a long time, near and far, high and low, higher than the deep forests, lower than the high clouds, until they reached the white-stoned royal palace. Ivan rode through the iron gates into the courtyard, tied his horse to the silver pillar and sat the babbling tom-cat on it. Then he went straight through the gold doors into the palace, bowing to the guards, but saying nothing. The guards were thinking:

"We haven't seen this old woman for a long time."

Inside the palace Ivan soon found the sleeping Princess Blue-eyes. He tiptoed to her side, and took from under her right cheek the eyes belonging to his father, Bel Belanin. The princess was so beautiful that Ivan leant over her and kissed her sugary lips. Then he hastened away, taking the babbling tom-cat from the gold pillar, and unhitching his horse. He leapt into the saddle and rode off. The horse spoke to him in a human voice, "You should never have kissed the princess on her sugary lips. You will pay for it now."

The horse was quite right. When Ivan kissed Blue-eyes on her sugary lips, she woke up and realized her visitor was Ivan and that he had taken from under her right cheek the eyes belonging to his father, Bel Belanin. Jumping up quickly, she sat on her heroic horse — and it happened to be the faster brother of Ivan's horse.

Ivan rode on and on, for a while and for a long time, near and far, high and low, higher than the dense forests, lower than the high clouds. Princess Blue-eyes was following.

As soon as Ivan came to Granny Jaga, she handed him a comb. "When Blue-eyes gets too near, toss this comb behind you and say: turn this wide open field into a thick forest."

Then the old woman handed him a stone. "The next time Blue-eyes gets too near, toss this stone behind you and say: turn this green meadow into a high mountain!"

Lastly she handed him a red hot cinder. "When Blue-eyes catches up with you again, toss this cinder behind you and say: let this flowing river turn to fire and all in its path burn!"

The moment Ivan left the cottage, Princess Blue-eyes entered. Granny Jaga nodded her head. "I welcome you here, maiden. Sit down and rest, I will prepare a bath for you."

"I haven't come to visit. I am chasing Ivan."

"Don't worry, he won't run away. You have the faster horse."

Granny Jaga cleaned the bath, lit the fire, boiled the water, and cleaned the birch brushes. It took a long time, for she was old and clumsy and everything fell from her hands. By the time Blue-eyes had steamed herself in the bath, Ivan was far away.

He rode on and on, for a while and for a long time, near and far, high and low, higher than the dense forests, lower than the high clouds. Princess Blue-eyes was hot on his heels.

Ivan looked round and saw that Princess Blue-eyes had nearly caught up with him.

IVAN AND PRINCESS
BLUE-EYES

She was waving the metal club, raising her very long lance, aiming her gun at him, brandishing her sharp sword. Ivan quickly threw behind him the comb the old woman had given him and said, "Turn this wide open field into a thick forest!"

Straight away a dense forest stood between Ivan and Blue-eyes. It was so thick no animal could pass through the thicket, no bird could fly through the branches. The maiden stopped, and with her sharp sword cleared a path to take her after Ivan.

Ivan looked round the second time and saw that Princess Blue-eyes had nearly caught up with him again. The metal club swung in the air, the long lance was fully raised, the gun aimed and her sword at the ready. Ivan quickly threw the stone Granny Jaga had given him behind him and said, "Turn this green meadow into a high mountain!"

Straight away a high mountain made of solid rock stood between Ivan and Blue-eyes. It was so hard and smooth, a snake could not climb it, and so high, no bird could fly over it. Blue-eyes stopped, raised her metal club and with one fierce stroke broke the mountain in half and galloped away after Ivan through the opening.

When Ivan looked round the third time, he saw the maiden hot on his heels. The metal club swung in the air, the long lance was raised, the gun well aimed and the sword at the ready. Ivan threw the burning cinder from Granny Jaga behind him, and said:

"Let this flowing river turn to fire and all in its path burn!"

Straight away a burning river flowed between Ivan and the girl. A fish could not have survived in it, a mosquito could not have flown across it. Blue-eyes came to a halt and thought hard. The metal club was useless against a burning river, so was the extra long lance, and the sharp sword, even the gun. Her heroic horse could not swim across, nor jump across. So she took a very deep breath and blew as fiercely as a gale, clearing a path through the flames and galloped away after Ivan.

Ivan turned round again and realized he could not get away from Blue-eyes. He jumped off his horse and faced the maiden, who called to him, "You cannot escape me, Ivan! Now we shall charge against each other from a distance of a horse's three leaps, a horse's three steps and we shall see who is the better of us two."

They charged from the distance of a horse's three leaps, a horse's three steps, raising their metal clubs, extra long lances and sharp swords. They met so violently that sparks flew, but both remained seated. They rode against each other again and again; both stayed firm in their saddle. When they met for the third time, Ivan's horse stumbled and threw his master from the saddle. Princess Blue-eyes jumped to the ground, knelt across Ivan's chest and began to remove his steel armour. She wanted to cut open his chest and pierce his heart.

Ivan said to her, "Don't take my armour off, dear princess, don't pierce my white flesh with your sword! Kiss me on the lips instead."

Blue-eyes stopped taking the armour off; she did not stick her sword into Ivan's chest, but kissed him on his lips instead.

Then they put up a white tent in the meadow and for three weeks they enjoyed each other's company, for three weeks they celebrated and held a wedding.

After the three weeks they bade each other goodbye. Princess Blue-eyes said to Ivan, "I will come in three years time to fetch you from your father, Czar Bel Belanin."

Then they parted.

Ivan returned home, went to his father, Czar Bel Belanin, pushed his eyes back in their place and sprinkled him with the water of death. The eyes grew back into their sockets, but the Czar stopped breathing. So Ivan sprinkled him with the water of life and the Czar woke up and his sight was better than ever before. He embraced his son Ivan and said, "Thank you, my son, for making me well again and for giving me back my sight. Because of this you will be Czar after my death and your elder brothers will be as your younger brothers and will have to obey you."

Fjodor and Vasilij grumbled about this and whispered to everyone, "What a Czardom it will be, what a kingdom, with young Ivan as our Czar! That will be our downfall, that will be our shame! We shall be the laughing stock of our enemies."

Eventually they said all this to the Czar himself and he was now sorry that he had promised Ivan the Czarship.

All this reached Ivan's ears, and he was upset that his brothers were so envious and his father so ungrateful. Without saying goodbye, he saddled his horse and rode out into the world to see new faces and fresh places and to forget how they had wronged him. He was away three long years, and no one in his Czardom heard news of him, nor saw him.

At the end of the third year a magnificent gold vessel sailed into port by the Czar's palace. Princess Blue-eyes stepped ashore, accompanied by her two sons — children of her husband Ivan. She sent messengers to Czar Bel Belanin asking for his son.

Czar Bel Belanin was afraid of Princess Blue-eyes, so he sent to her his son Fjodor.

"Is this our father?" asked the sons.

"No, it is your unkind uncle," answered their mother.

With that the two boys threw Fjodor into the water. He very nearly drowned and was fished out of the sea dripping wet and very much ashamed.

Czar Bel Belanin sent Vasilij next.

"Is this our father?" asked the boys.

"No, it is another unkind uncle of yours," said the mother.

The two boys threw Vasilij into the sea. He too very nearly drowned and was fished out dripping wet, feeling sick with shame.

At that moment Ivan arrived upon his heroic horse. He bowed deeply before Blue-eyes, kissed her upon her sugary lips, and embraced the children.

"This is your kind father," said the Princess to their sons. They took him by the hand and led him to the gold vessel.

Then they sailed to the Czardom of Princess Blue-eyes, to her white marble palace. They held a great feast to celebrate and it lasted for three whole months, three weeks and three days. Everyone came from all the nation, to dance, to be merry, day and night, to taste wines and food. What a sight! What a feast! What a celebration!

IVAN AND PRINCESS
BLUE-EYES

THE ARTFUL FOX

Once there was a forest where a pine tree stood among the heather. Under the pine a rabbit was fast asleep, and in its branches a squirrel was hopping about merrily. It was busily taking the seeds of the fir cones and throwing the peeled shells on the ground. One peeled cone fell smack on the rabbit's nose. It jumped up, pricking its ears, and cried, "The world is crumbling, the skies are falling down!" and it scurried away.

"Why are you running away, rabbit?" the squirrel called after it.

"The world is crumbling, the skies are falling down; you had better run too!"

The squirrel jumped off the tree and ran on with the rabbit. They met a swine, "Why are you running away, rabbit and squirrel?"

"The world is crumbling, the skies are falling down; you had better run too!" cried the rabbit. The swine caught them up and ran on with them.

The wolf saw them. "Why are you running away, rabbit, with the squirrel and the swine?"

"The world is crumbling, the skies are falling down; you had better run too!"

So the wolf joined them. Then a fox caught up with them. "Why are you running away, rabbit, with the squirrel, the swine and the wolf?"

"The world is crumbling, the skies are falling down; you had better run too!"

So the fox also joined them. They ran on and on, not caring where they went. Suddenly the rabbit tripped over some straw and they all tumbled down a deep, steep hollow: the rabbit, the squirrel, the swine, the wolf and the fox.

They all sat in the hollow feeling extremely hungry, but there was nothing at all to eat. The fox suggested, "It is no good, friends, we'll just have to sing. We'll eat the one with the highest voice for our dinner."

The wolf sang in its deep voice o-o-o, the swine's voice was lower with its oo-oo-oo, the fox sang aa-aa-aa, but the poor rabbit and poor squirrel could only manage a high pitched i-i-i. So they were gobbled up.

The next day the fox said, "We'll sing again. This time we'll eat the one with the deepest voice."

The fox sang aa-aa-aa, the wolf a deep o-o-o and the swine a very low oo-oo-oo. Its voice was definitely the lowest one, so it too was eaten up.

As the swine was very fat, the fox couldn't quite manage it all. So it hid the swine's tongue for the next time.

The following morning the fox started eating the swine's tongue.

"What are you eating, foxie?" asked the wolf.

"As I am hungry, I have bitten off my own tongue and am eating it," lied the fox.

The wolf was hungry too, so it bit off its own tongue, but the poor thing choked itself to death with it! So the fox ate the wolf too.

Now the fox really had nothing else to eat.

Over the hollow grew a beech tree, where a thrush had built its nest. As it fluttered around, the fox called to it, "What are you doing, thrush?"

"I am mending my nest."

"Why are you mending it?" the fox asked.

"Because my children are growing."

"Now listen, thrush, pull me out of this hollow, otherwise I'll gobble up all your children."

The thrush gathered branches and threw them into the hollow. The pile grew and grew, until the fox could climb out.

"You helped me out of the hollow, didn't you, thrush?" the fox called, when it was safely on top.

"That I did, foxie," said the thrush.

"Now you must feed me, otherwise I'll gobble up all your children," the fox ordered.

The thrush flew to a field, the fox following on the ground. A young girl was walking along, taking bread, butter and cakes to the harvesters. The thrush hopped about in the field, dragging one of its wings behind it, as if it was broken. The girl put her basket down and ran after the bird, trying to catch it. The thrush fluttered further, the little girl followed and the artful fox in the meantime crept to the basket and helped itself to all the farm workers' lunches! It really enjoyed the food too!

"You helped me out of the hollow, didn't you, thrush?" the fox said a while later.

"That I did, foxie."

"You fed me too, didn't you?"

"That I did."

"Now find me something to drink, otherwise I'll gobble up all your children."

The thrush flew over the road, the fox followed.

A farmer was wheeling a barrow with a barrel of wine. The thrush perched upon the barrel and pecked at the tap. The farmer picked a stone, threw it at the bird, but knocked the tap off. Wine started to flow from the barrel and the farmer was so mad, he pushed the barrel off the barrow and went home empty handed. The fox drank and drank, until its stomach was like a barrel.

"You helped me out of the hollow, didn't you, thrush?" it said later on.

"That I did, foxie."

"You fed me too?"

"That I did."

"And you quenched my thirst?"

"I did."

"Now make me laugh, otherwise I'll gobble up all your children."

The thrush flew into the village and the fox followed. Behind a hedge a farmer and his wife were threshing corn.

The bird perched upon the woman's head.

"Stand still and don't move!" the farmer cried and swung his flail with all his might. Crash! it went, but the thrush had flown away and the wife had the full blast upon her head. It knocked her clean over! Fuming with fury, she seized a pail of slops and threw it at her husband. The farmer, waving his flail, chased his wife, who ran all over the village shouting, "Help me, folk, the farmer wants to beat me to death!"

The fox laughed until tears ran down its hairy cheeks.

"Did you help me out of the hollow, thrush?"

"That I did, foxie."

"Did you feed me too?"

"I did that also."

"And did you quench my thirst?"

"I did."

"And did you make me laugh?"

"I made you laugh."

"Now make me afraid, otherwise I'll gobble up all your children."

The thrush turned further into the village, the fox followed. The bird perched upon a cottage gate and cried, "Raggy taggy granny, you are an ugly old hag, dressed in a sack!"

The old woman opened her door and sent her hounds after the bird. But as soon as they caught the scent of the fox, they left the thrush alone and pursued the fox. The fox ran away and only just managed to escape by slipping into a hole.

After the fox had got over the shock, it said, "What did you do, my ears, whilst I was running?"

"We were on the alert, so the dogs would not catch you."

"For that I will buy you a pair of ear-rings. What did you do, my eyes, whilst I was running?"

"We watched our way carefully, so you could run fast and not be caught."

"For that I will buy you a pretty pair of glasses. And what about you, my feet, what did you do whilst I was on the run?"

"We ran away as fast as we could, jumping over tree stumps and boulders, so the hounds wouldn't get you."

"For that I will buy you a nice pair of shoes. And you, my tail, what did you do whilst I was on the run?"

"I got in the way of your back legs, and tried to wrap myself round the tree stumps and boulders, so the hounds would catch you and eat you up!"

"Well I never!" cried the fox indignantly.

"Here you are, hounds, you can have this horrid tail," and it pushed its tail out of the hole. The hounds bit it off and ate it and the fox was left tailless.

THE ARTFUL FOX

All the animals laughed at the fox without a tail, even the tiny baby rabbits, and this really annoyed the fox.

"Really, it isn't important that I haven't a tail," the fox said to them one day. "But you should see how beautifully I can dance round and round."

The little rabbits wanted to know how to dance round and round. They begged the fox to show them, or to teach them.

"You'll have to tie your tails together first."

"We don't know how to. Will you do it for us?" the baby rabbits asked.

The fox then tied their tails together and cried, "Beware, rabbits, beware! The wolf is coming to get you!"

The terrified rabbits pulled and shoved this way and that way; they shoved and they pulled until they tore their tails right out. So the artful foxie had the last laugh of all.

All this happened in days of old, when tails were as scarce as solid pure gold.

THE DAZZLING
FALCON FINISTER

In Millionth Street of St. Petersburg there once lived a wealthy merchant Terenin. who had three daughters. The two eldest ones were good looking and proud, the youngest one Maria was modest, hardworking and a real beauty.

When one day merchant Terenin set out on his business travels, he asked his daughters, "What would you like me to bring you back?"

The two eldest sisters asked for expensive dresses, shoes and jewellery, but the youngest one said, "Please father, bring me a feather from the dazzling falcon Finister."

The merchant was surprised to hear such a strange wish, but he promised to return with everything his daughters asked for.

Some time later the father was on his way home. He bought beautiful dresses, shoes and jewellery, but he had been unable to find the feather from the dazzling falcon Finister.

Just before he entered St. Petersburg he met an aged, bent man. The merchant said in greeting, "Good health to you, grandfather!"

"Good health to you too, merchant Terenin! You are returning home, but you do not seem very happy."

"That is true, grandfather! My youngest daughter Maria asked me to bring her the feather from the dazzling falcon Finister, but I could not find it anywhere."

The old man nodded his head and said, "I have such a feather, and it is a very rare feather. It is not for sale. As you are a kind man, however, I will give it to you for nothing."

Then the old man gave the merchant an ordinary looking, tiny feather.

Merchant Terenin went on happily home. He gave his eldest daughters the expensive dresses, shoes and jewellery, Maria's gift was the feather of the dazzling falcon Finister.

The eldest sisters straight away dressed up in their new finery, preened themselves in the mirror and laughed at silly Maria. Maria did not care! She went into her own room, threw the feather on the floor and, lo and behold! The small feather first turned into a dazzling falcon and then into a handsome youth.

Maria and her Finister stayed together happily all night long; at break of dawn the handsome youth turned again into a falcon and flew away out of Maria's window.

From that day the dazzling falcon Finister visited Maria every night. He flew into her room in the evening, turned into the handsome youth, stayed all night and then flew away again at the crack of dawn, in the form of the falcon.

Her sisters soon noticed that a dazzling falcon was flying to Maria and they began to tell tales to their father. He said abruptly, "Daughters, why don't you mind your own business?"

The elder sisters were jealous of Maria, so they set a snare for the falcon by glueing sharp fragments of glass on her window and gave Maria a large dose of a sleeping draught. The dazzling falcon Finister vainly tried to enter Maria's room that night; vainly tried to wake her up by knocking on the window with his beak. His chest was torn and bleeding from the sharp glass, but Maria was in a deep sleep.

In the end falcon Finister cried out, "Whoever really needs me, will find me, but it will be difficult. He or she will have to look for me for a long, long time, until three pairs of iron shoes are worn out, three iron walking sticks are broken, and three iron hats are torn. Then I will be found."

By then Maria was recovering from her drugged sleep and heard the falcon's words. She rushed to the window and flung it wide open, but her dear one had already flown away. A few drops of blood on the window sill was all that was left of him. Maria cried bitterly and her tears washed away the drops of blood. Then she prepared herself for the long journey. She ordered three pairs of iron shoes, three iron walking sticks and three iron hats, bade her father goodbye and left home.

Maria travelled a long, long time, over really rough ground. It may sound easy in a story, but in real life it was very hard. She had already worn out one pair of the iron shoes, broken one of the iron walking sticks and torn one of the iron hats, when she came to a clearing in the middle of a deep forest, where a small cottage stood. Maria entered and saw a white-haired old man sitting by the stove.

"What brings you here, maiden? I have been sitting by this stove for a hundred years now, and have not seen a single soul."

"I am searching for my sweetheart, for my falcon Finister, grandfather," answered Maria.

The old man nodded his head, but he knew nothing of such a falcon.

"Wait here till morning, young maiden. All the woodland creatures gather on this clearing at dawn; perhaps they may have news of your sweetheart."

Maria spent the night in the cottage and at dawn, just like the old man said, all the woodland creatures gathered in the clearing. There were bears, wolves, deer, even the tiniest ants, but they knew nothing about falcon Finister.

"I am sorry, Maria, that I cannot help you," said the old man. "But at least I will give you a present. Take this silver tray with the golden egg. When you put the tray down, the egg will start rolling on its own. You must not sell the tray for anything, except for one night with falcon Finister. Now one of the deer will lead you out of the forest. Follow the sun until you come to the blue sea. My elder brother lives there, maybe he will be able to help you."

The deer led Maria out of the forest and she followed the sun, walking on and on, over rough ground. It was harder in real life than it sounds in a story.

When she wore out the second pair of shoes, when she broke the second iron walking stick, when she tore the second iron hat, she came to the blue sea. A tiny cottage stood right on the shore. Maria entered and found an aged, white-haired man by the stove.

"Welcome to you, maiden," he said in greeting. "What brings you here? I have sat by this stove for three hundred years now, without seeing a living soul."

Maria replied:

"I am looking for my sweetheart, falcon Finister, dear grandfather."

But the old man had never heard of falcon Finister.

"Wait here till morning, young maiden. All the sea creatures gather by the shore at dawn; perhaps one of them might know something about your dearest one."

Maria stayed in the cottage overnight and as the old man said, all the sea creatures swam to the shore the following morning; there were big fish and little fish, seals, sea horses and even tiny sprats. But they knew nothing about the dazzling falcon Finister.

"I am afraid I cannot help you," said the old man. "I will at least give you a present. Take this gold loom with the silver spinning wheel. The wheel will weave a thin, gold thread on its own. But you must not sell it to anyone, not for anything, except for one night with falcon Finister. Now this whale will take you across the sea, then you must walk on and on until you climb the white mountain, where my eldest brother lives in his cottage. Maybe he will be able to help."

Maria rode across the sea on the whale's back, and then walked on and on, over rough ground. It was much harder in real life than it is to tell in a fairy story. When she wore out the third pair of iron shoes, when she broke the third iron walking stick, when she tore the third iron hat, she saw the tiny cottage on the white mountain. She went inside and found a white-haired old man resting by the stove. He said in greeting, "Good health to you, young maiden! What brings you here? I have been resting by this stove for one thousand years now, and have not seen a single living soul."

"I am searching for my beloved, for falcon Finister," Maria replied.

Even the eldest old man knew nothing about Finister.

"Never mind, stay here till morning. All the birds assemble here then and maybe one of them will know something about your sweetheart."

At dawn the next day all the birds really did gather in front of the cottage — eagles, hawks, everything that flew, right down to the tiniest moth. They too knew nothing about falcon Finister. Suddenly a swish of wings was heard and an enormous falcon flew to the ground. He said, "Falcon Finister is my brother and he is in a crystal castle a thousand miles from here. The countess who lives there has captured him and is feeding him with the wine of forgetfulness, for she wants to have him for a husband."

When Maria heard that the countess from the crystal castle intended to wed her beloved, she began to weep bitterly. The old man tried to cheer her up:

"Do not grieve, dear maiden! You will see everything will end happily. The falcon will fly you down the mountain and you will go on to the castle. Take with you this silver frame with the gold needle. When you put the frame down, the needle will embroider a silk scarf all on its own. But do not sell the frame for anything but one night with falcon Finister."

The falcon took Maria down the mountain and she walked on and on, over rough ground. She had no shoes left, no walking stick and no hat. Her bare feet were torn by sharp stones until they bled. She used her hands to support herself against the trees. The hot sun burnt her bare head. Then at last Maria came to the crystal castle.

The maiden sat on the crystal doorstep of the castle and took out of her bag the silver tray with the gold egg. When she put them on the floor, the egg began to roll all over the place. People gathered to see this strange sight.

The countess who reigned in this crystal castle, saw the crowd of people, and sent her maid to find out what was going on. The maid soon returned with the tale about the magic egg made of gold, which rolled about all on its own and which with its silver tray belonged to a girl called Maria, who refused to sell it for anything but one night spent with falcon Finister.

The countess simply waved her hand and said to the maid, "Run and fetch the silver tray with the gold egg! Tell the girl to come in the evening, then I will take her to falcon Finister. It won't bring her any joy, for after taking the wine of forgetfulness, falcon Finister sleeps like the dead and no one wakes him up."

So Maria came to her beloved at last. She stood over him all night long, whispering sweet words of love, but Finister slept on, knowing and hearing nothing. The next morning Maria left in tears.

Once again she sat on the crystal step of the crystal castle. This time she took out the gold loom with the silver spinning wheel which spun a gold thread on its own. People crowded around to see this miracle. The countess sent her maid down again to find out what was happening. When afterwards the maid told her of the gold loom and the silver spinning wheel which spun a gold thread on its own, and that Maria would sell for nothing less than a night with falcon Finister, the countess sent her back with a wave of her hand, "Go and fetch the loom and the wheel! Tell the girl to come here again this evening, but she won't wake Finister!"

Poor Maria once again tried all night in vain to wake her beloved with sweet words of love. He slept like the dead, without flickering even an eyelid.

The only thing Maria now had left was the silver tray and the gold needle. She sat on the crystal doorstep of the crystal castle, while the needle embroidered a silk scarf with a gold thread all on its own. People ran to her side to witness this miracle. The countess again sent her maid to see what all the commotion was about. When she was told that Maria now had a silver frame with a silk scarf, which a gold needle was embroidering with a silver thread all on its own, and that Maria refused to sell except for one night with falcon Finister, the countess laughed and said, "Go and bring the silver frame and the gold needle! I will gladly leave her another night with Finister. After all, it will be the last time, for tomorrow is our wedding day."

The unhappy Maria spent the last night with Finister. In vain she tried to wake her beloved with sweet words of love. Finister slept like the dead. When dawn was breaking and the night ending, Maria burst into tears and one of her tears dropped on Finister's

THE DAZZLING
FALCON FINISTER

forehead. Then something incredible and wonderful happened. As the tear touched his white forehead, Finister moved, opened his eyes and looked at Maria. And he cried joyfully, "So you found me after all, darling Maria! You have worn out three pairs of iron shoes, broken three iron walking sticks, torn three iron hats, and now broken the evil, magic spell."

With that he kissed the happy Maria on her sweet lips.

A wedding was held that day. Finister was not marrying the wicked countess, but his kind, gentle Maria. It was a truly happy wedding, because true love had won. So this tale has a happy ending after all.

THE ARTFUL SOLDIER
AND THE CZAR'S
THREE DAUGHTERS

The sparrow flew swiftly, just as an arrow, across the sea from east to west, till in a far away land it came to rest. In this land there was a Czardom and in this Czardom a Czar and his Czarina reigned. They had three daughters and the whole family lived together happily. That was, until the eldest daughter reached her seventeenth birthday.

On that fateful day she asked her parents if she could go for a stroll in the castle gardens. The parents gave their permission. The daughter, in the company of her nurses and maids, was walking in the grounds, laughing and talking to the others — when suddenly, she was gone! The nurses and maids called and searched for the princess all over the place, but it was no use. She had disappeared. The Czar and the Czarina rushed into the gardens with all their servants. They searched every corner, every bush, but the princess was nowhere to be seen. It was as if the ground had opened and swallowed her up.

Now the Czar and the Czarina were left with only two daughters.

Time passed quickly and soon the second daughter was celebrating her seventeenth birthday. She too begged her parents to be allowed out into the castle gardens. Naturally they did not want her to go. They recalled only too well how their eldest daughter had disappeared. But the second daughter kept on pleading, so in the end they gave their permission, but made her promise she would not hide anywhere nor stay alone even for a minute. The princess therefore took with her all her personal maids and nurses. They strolled through the grounds, laughing, talking and joking — when suddenly, the daughter was gone!

Now the poor Czar and the Czarina only had one daughter left, the youngest one. They loved and cared for her as if she was a china doll, fussing round her all day long.

Soon she too celebrated her seventeenth birthday and pleaded with her parents to be allowed to take a stroll in the castle gardens. The Czar would not hear of it at first, though his daughter begged and begged for his permission. In the end it was the Czarina herself who came to her daughter's rescue, saying she personally would accompany her and look after her. Then at last the Czar agreed. But all this was still of no use. There was a sudden gust of wind — and the princess was gone! She disappeared like a mist before the sun and no one knew where she had gone.

The Czar was grief-stricken, the Czarina wept wherever she went and the whole Czardom was in mourning. The Czar announced that any person who would find just one of his daughters, would gain her as a bride and in addition get half of his kingdom.

Many men searched for the princesses, but no one had any idea where to start looking, and people were afraid it might be the work of some evil magic. Then one day a General came to the Czar and said, "Your Highness! I want to try my luck. Perhaps I will bring you back one daughter at last. Give me a regiment of soldiers and five thousand roubles and I will set off tomorrow."

The Czar was very pleased to give him what he asked for; no price was too high to pay for a daughter.

The next morning the General and his men marched out in great style to look for the princesses. They marched until they came to an inn at the other end of the town.

"Company halt!" the General cried. "We'll rest a while here. Company, fall out!"

The soldiers sat down in front of the inn and their General went inside. The inn-keeper placed before him the very best food and wines he had, and then said, "Would you care for a game of cards, dear General, whilst your soldiers are resting?"

"With pleasure," was the reply.

The inn-keeper dealt the cards, they played a few hands and very soon the General lost the five thousand roubles which the Czar had given him, all the regiment of soldiers, his sword and his uniform — and he still owed more! So the inn-keeper locked the General and his troops in a sty and the poor Czar vainly waited for their return.

When the General failed to come back for a long time, another General went to see the Czar. This one asked for ten thousand roubles and two regiments of soldiers. The Czar was again only too pleased to give him what he asked; no price was too high to pay for the return of a daughter.

The next morning the General and his men marched out in great style to look for the princesses. They marched on and on, until they came to the very same inn where the first General had lost everything — including himself, in a game of cards.

This General also entered the inn, started to play cards with the inn-keeper and after playing a while, lost the ten thousand roubles the Czar had given him, all his soldiers, sword and uniform — and he still owed more! So the inn-keeper locked him and his troops in the same sty which housed the first General. The poor Czar waited in vain for the return of at least one of his Generals.

A certain soldier served in the castle who was as cunning as a fox. One day he reported to the Czar, "Your Highness! The Generals did not get very far, so now I shall go to find your daughters."

"But you are just an ordinary soldier," grumbled the Czar.

"That may be so. Just give me twenty roubles and I will start in the morning!"

The Czar did not like the idea at all. What could a common soldier achieve where two Generals with whole regiments had failed? Then he decided there was really no harm in trying, and that he would have a clear conscience if he gave the soldier what he asked for. The soldier, with the twenty roubles in his pocket, set off.

He walked on and on, until he came to the far end of the town, to the inn where both the Generals had played cards. He went straight in and ordered bread and cheese. The inn-keeper was out, and his daughter was serving and she asked the soldier where he was going.

(146) 147   THE ARTFUL SOLDIER
AND THE CZAR'S THREE DAUGHTERS

"I am searching for the Czar's daughters. The Generals have gone before me with whole regiments of soldiers, but they have disappeared just like water from the basket."

The inn-keeper's daughter, hearing those words, was doubled up with laughter.

"What is so funny?" asked the soldier.

"The joke is that both the Generals and all their soldiers are locked up in our sty. My father put them there."

Then the maiden went on to tell how her father had beaten them both at cards. The soldier, nodding his head, said, "What I can't understand is why those Generals kept losing. Our Generals are real card sharpers!"

"That may be so, but our father has a magic chair. Whoever sits in it always wins."

"Which chair is it?"

"The one you are sitting on."

They dropped the subject then. The soldier ordered something to drink and waited for the inn-keeper's arrival. He came in the evening, and as soon as he saw the soldier, he took the cards out, hoping to have a hand or two.

"Why not?" the soldier agreed with a wave of his hand. "But I don't know how to play."

"Don't worry, you will soon learn," the inn-keeper remarked. "But let me sit on my chair, I am used to it now."

The soldier had no intention of getting off the magic seat, so he replied:

"I am not moving! I am very comfortable."

What could the inn-keeper do? Then he thought that as the soldier knew nothing about cards, he would beat him easily, even if he had been sitting on two magic chairs. He dealt the cards. The cunning soldier, of course, really knew how to play and he won game after game. He won back all the Generals' money, then all the soldiers, next both the Generals — in all, the inn-keeper lost everything.

"I warn you, friend," the soldier smiled mockingly, "next time don't start anything with soldiers!"

The soldier let the regiments of troops out of the sty and sent them back to the castle. Then he turned to the Generals. "Now, young fellows, pull yourselves together, for we are going in search of the princesses."

The Generals did not want to go, but there was nothing else for it. The soldier had won them in a game of cards, so they had to obey him. Obediently, they followed.

They walked on and on until they reached a certain town just on market day. But it was really a strange market. All the stalls were empty, there was nothing for sale, except for one stall, where a rope maker was selling rope.

"I suppose a good piece of rope could come in useful," the soldier thought, and bought one hundred yards of the thickest and strongest rope. He gave it to his Generals to carry and they walked on.

They came to an overgrown gorge. At the very bottom of it was a deep hollow.

"I think we had better investigate what is inside, young fellows," said the soldier.

"I will tie one end of the rope round my waist, and you must let me down the hollow. Wait until I pull the rope three times, then haul me up again. Do you understand?"

What a deep, fathomless hollow it was. The rope was only just long enough. To the soldier's surprise it opened up into a beautiful glade and in the centre stood a magnificent castle built of lead. The soldier stepped inside and came face to face with none other than the Czar's eldest daughter.

"How happy I am to see you," said the princess. "Who has ever seen anyone, or heard of anyone wandering right down here? Even wild beasts and daring rooks avoid this place, and yet you have come!"

"I have come from your father, the Czar, to take you back home," explained the soldier.

"How can you take me home when I am guarded by the three-headed dragon? He will fly down any moment now and gobble you up."

"Maybe he'll eat me up, maybe I'll finish him off," bragged the soldier.

The Czar's daughter grew pensive, then said, "I know how I can help. The dragon keeps two bottles in this closet. On the right is the water of strength, on the left the water of weakness. As soon as he arrives, he will sense your presence. But have no fear, soldier. Go and meet him and speak with him. He will drink from the bottle on the right and will give you the one on the left. But I will have changed them over, so he will grow weaker and you stronger. Then you will be able to fight him."

The Czar's daughter did as she had said. Soon the dragon flew down. Enormous, frightening eyes rolled in his repulsive three heads. As he came through the gates he roared, "What do you want here? Wild beasts dare not come here, rooks would not fly here, but you — a simple soldier — have come. What are you looking for?"

"It is none of your business. Actually I have come for the princess. It is time she returned home."

"How dare you speak to me like that!" the dragon fumed, blowing out fiery smoke through all of his three noses. "I'll have you for my dinner right away."

"Maybe you will, but maybe I'll be the death of you."

The dragon was somewhat taken aback by such courageous words, so he tried another approach. "Shall there be a fight between us, or peace between us, or even brotherhood between us?"

"We'll have the fight," said the soldier. "I haven't come down this terrible hollow just to be friends."

"Let's drink to it first!" the dragon suggested.

"Give me a bottle then!" said the soldier.

The dragon opened the closet and took both of the bottles out. He gave a drink to the soldier from the one on the left, and had a drink himself from the one on the right. He had no idea that the bottles had been switched round. Strength seeped into the soldier's body, but drained away from the dragon.

"Let us begin!" the dragon roared.

"You can start!"

The dragon brandished his terrible sword, but the soldier jumped aside as it came down and it cut into the floor with such force, the dragon fell right over. The soldier then, with one clean swipe of his sword, severed all the dragon's three heads. Afterwards he burnt the body and scattered the ashes into all four corners of the earth.

The princess could not thank the soldier enough for setting her free from the horrible dragon, but he was already preparing to go on to search for the second sister.

The princess said, "I know where to find my younger sister. She is not very far from here; she is in a silver castle and is guarded by a six-headed dragon."

She gave the soldier a lead egg and told him, "Put the egg into your other hand now!"

The soldier obeyed and as he did so, the lead castle vanished.

"When you want to build the castle again, just put the lead egg from one hand into the other."

The soldier thanked the princess, bade her goodbye and went on. He walked and walked till he reached the silver castle. As soon as he entered he met the second princess.

How surprised she was when she learned that the soldier had come to fetch her. Immediately she switched her two bottles over just as her eldest sister had done. Quite understandably it was then easy for the soldier to beat even the six-headed dragon. When the fight was over, the princess gave him a silver egg.

Now the soldier hurried to a golden castle to find the youngest princess, who was guarded by a nine-headed dragon. That fight proved more difficult, but as the princess had also switched the bottles over, he slew him in the end. This daughter gave the soldier a gold egg.

On their way back to the hollow they collected the second sister and then the eldest one.

How overjoyed they were to see each other! The soldier, however, was in a hurry to get out of the gorge. He was afraid the Generals might have tired of waiting. But they were there and as soon as he tied the rope round the eldest daughter of the Czar, and gave three tugs, they pulled her up, then the middle daughter and the youngest one too. They did not let the rope down for the soldier, but said to the three princesses instead, "Swear to us that you will tell your father the Czar that it was the two of us who saved you! Otherwise we shall kill you!"

What could the three sisters do? They begged and they wept, but in the end they gave their promise. The poor soldier remained in the hollow.

He soon realized that the Generals had double-crossed him. He scratched behind his ear, shrugged his shoulders and thought, "I had better make the best of it!"

Then he tossed the lead egg from one hand to the other — and the lead castle stood right before him. The soldier went inside and shouted, "Is anyone at home?"

A devil came out and asked, "What do you require?"

The soldier replied:

"Give me food and drink!"

As soon as he had spoken, a huge feast was set before him — all the delicious foods and wines, everything he could ask for. The soldier filled his belly and quenched his thirst and decided that it wasn't so bad, after all, to be left behind down the hollow. Then he took out the lead egg again, and made the lead castle disappear, and with the silver egg, he made the silver castle appear. The soldier went inside, shouting, "Is anyone at home?"

Two devils came out and asked, "What do you require?"

The soldier could not think what to ask for, so again he ordered something to eat and drink. And again, as soon as he had spoken, a lavish feast lay before him, even better than the previous one. He ate and drank so much he could not move afterwards. Then, with the gold egg, he made the gold castle appear. Once more he entered and shouted, "Anyone at home?"

A whole procession of devils came and they all asked, "What do you require?"

The soldier replied:

"I want some food and drink!"

No sooner said than done, and a feast was laid out before him, more lavish than both the previous ones. The best foods, the best wines; all he could wish for. But the soldier was too full to eat even a single mouthful, to down even a single sip of wine. He sat at the table and gazed sadly at all the splendour.

A gold balalaika was hanging above the table. The soldier, feeling a little bored, took it down and played a tune. Immediately the whole procession of devils reappeared, and they all cried and begged the soldier to return the balalaika to them. They had forgotten it in the castle and would be greatly punished in hell if they did not come back with it in one piece. They were so anxious to get the instrument, they promised heaven and earth for its return.

"All right then," said the soldier cunningly. "I will give you back your balalaika, if you first take me out of the hollow."

The devils were only too eager to oblige and immediately they stood one on top of the other, forming a long ladder with their bodies. The soldier climbed up quite easily, said thank you nicely, gave the devil on top the balalaika, and went home.

When the soldier reached the town, he found lodgings in the suburbs with a poor old man.

The whole town was full of excitement, because two of the Czar's daughters were to be married. The two Generals, who claimed they were their rescuers, were to be their husbands. All the town talked of nothing else. In the castle too, there was a lot of joy and merriment. The Czar and his wife were so happy, they hardly knew what to do — only their daughters seemed somewhat sad. They came to the Czar and the youngest one said, "Father, dear, ask those gallant Generals who brought us home to bring us also silk stockings exactly like the ones we wore in the other world down the hollow."

The Czar was surprised to hear such a strange request, but then he thought that such a small task would be easy for the Generals to perform.

THE ARTFUL SOLDIER
AND THE CZAR'S THREE DAUGHTERS

But where were the Generals to find silk stockings, like the ones the Czar's daughters wore in the other world? They searched the whole town, asking everyone whether they knew about such stockings, but nobody could help or advise them. All this reached the ears of our cunning soldier and he said to the old man with whom he lived, "Grandfather, run after the Generals and tell them that you will knit them the stockings they require by tomorrow morning. But don't be shy and quote them a high price!"

The old man found the Generals and said, "Good health to you, Generals! I have heard that you are looking for silk stockings, such as the ones the princesses wore in the other world."

"That is so, grandfather. Do you know where we can get them?"

"I most certainly do. If you wish, I will knit some for you by morning."

"Really?" cried the overjoyed Generals. "How much do you want for them?"

"Three thousand roubles."

"Three thousand roubles, that is quite a tidy sum. Oh, never mind, it is worth half the Czardom!" the Generals agreed and gave the money to the old man. "But make sure the stockings are here by tomorrow morning!"

As soon as the old man returned, the soldier asked how he got on. The old man truthfully told him that he had been given three thousand roubles.

"That's good. Now we can go to bed."

"And who is going to knit the stockings?" asked the old man worriedly.

"Don't give them another thought. In any case, you won't have to knit them."

The soldier was first to awake in the morning.

Quickly he tossed all the three eggs from one hand to the other and in the lead castle, silver castle and gold castle he soon found the pairs of silk stockings belonging to the Czar's daughters. Then he made the castles disappear again and shook the old man.

"Get up, grandfather, it is time to go! Here are the silk stockings! Now take them to the Generals."

The old man was so astonished, his eyes nearly fell out of his head! He could not understand where the stockings had come from, but he asked no questions and took them to the Generals.

"Are you sure these are exactly the same as those worn by the princesses in the other, hollow world?" asked the Generals.

"They are the same," grandfather answered and went home.

The Generals handed the stockings to the Czar and he gave them to his daughters.

"These really are the same as those we wore in the other, hollow world," they agreed. The youngest daughter said, "As these gallant Generals were able to bring us silk stockings, let them now bring us the same velvet slippers as we wore in our other, hollow world."

Where else could the Generals hope to find such slippers, but at the old man's house? But they did not know where he lived. The Generals searched the town, asking everyone. The cunning soldier heard about this and sent the old man after them.

"But this time ask for more than three thousand!" he told him.

The old man asked for four thousand roubles, and got them! The soldier then found the velvet slippers in the lead castle, the silver castle, and the gold castle. The Generals did not even stop to ask if they were exactly the same as those worn by the Czar's daughters in the other, hollow world, but rushed back to the Czar. The Czar gave the slippers to his daughters, who were really astonished:

"They truly are exactly the same as those we wore in the other, hollow world."

The youngest daughter said:

"As these gallant Generals were able to bring us our velvet slippers which we wore in the other, hollow world, let them now build us by morning the castles we lived in there."

This request seemed too much for the Czar.

"Are you crazy?" he asked angrily. "Those two men are Generals! They could probably knock a castle or two down by morning, but build one, never! You can't ask them to do that."

But the sisters stubbornly insisted, saying they had a good reason for doing so and that it was not just some silly whim. The Czar had no option but to call the Generals and order them to build the three castles.

They were really astounded to be given such an enormous task, but the old man came to their rescue, offering to complete the job by morning for ten thousand roubles.

Ten thousand roubles was too much even for Generals, but what else could they do? Half a Czardom was worth the price. So they parted with the money and the old man went home.

"How did you get on?" asked the soldier eagerly.

"Very well. I was given ten thousand roubles."

"Come on, grandfather, let's celebrate!"

They sauntered to the very best inn of the town, where only noblemen, counts and countesses normally went. There the soldier and the old man feasted till dawn.

When the sun was rising, they paid their bill and walked to the Czar's castle. The soldier tossed all the three eggs from hand to hand, and in a trice three castles stood before them, one built of lead, one built of silver, one built of gold. The turrets of all the castles sparkled and glistened; they dazzled the eye.

The three castles glowed so fiercely that the brightness woke all the Czar's family. The Czar, the Czarina and their three daughters ran to inspect the magnificent sight, and so did all the servants and attendants.

Only the Generals stayed inside. Their rooms faced the opposite side, so they did not see the glow.

When the Czar and his daughters came over to the three castles, they found the soldier and the old man sitting on one doorstep. The youngest princess ran to him, took him by the hand and led him to the Czar. "This is the real hero, daddy! This is the man who saved us, and not those two Generals!"

(154) 155   THE ARTFUL SOLDIER

AND THE CZAR'S THREE DAUGHTERS

The other two princesses nodded their heads in agreement and explained to their father what had happened and how they were forced to swear they would not tell the truth, otherwise they would have been killed. The Czar was very angry to hear this and gave the order for the Generals to be pulled out of their beds and driven out of town.

The cunning soldier was given the youngest daughter for a bride and half the Czardom as well. They held a wonderful wedding, more splendid than in most fairy stories. Everyone ate and drank so much, they were fit to burst and I am only fit to rest now, so this is the end of this tale.

THE BRIDES OF THE BEAR

In a tiny cottage in a green meadow there lived an old man and an old woman with their three daughters. Beyond the meadow, in the deep forest, there lived in another cottage a hairy, furry bear. He had a cat with gold claws.

One day the bear said, "Cat with gold claws, find me a bride!"

The cat went to look for one. It climbed the fence of the cottage where the old man and the old woman lived with their three daughters. From the fence it jumped into the apple tree, from the apple tree into the cabbages. The eldest daughter saw it.

"Father, father, there's a cat in our garden with gold claws!"

"Catch it then!"

The girl ran outside. The cat jumped over the fence, the girl jumped over the fence; the cat ran along the path, the girl ran along the path; the cat leapt across the brook, the girl leapt across the brook; the cat went in the forest, the girl went into the forest; the cat entered the bear's cottage, the girl entered the bear's cottage.

The bear was sprawled on his bed, rubbing its paws with glee. "You've brought me a good housekeeper, cat with the gold claws! We'll be all right now. You, good woman, must cook for us and look after us. I will always bring you wood. Here are a set of keys. You can go into this cupboard and that one too, but if you open the third cupboard, I will kill you."

The next day the bear and the cat went for some wood. The girl opened the first cupboard and found bread. She opened the second cupboard, and found meat, lard and honey. But she could not resist looking into the third cupboard too. When she opened it, there were five tubs inside. She took the lid off the first tub and put her finger into it. The finger turned gold, for the tub was filled with gold water. The frightened girl quickly locked the cupboard, and bandaged her finger with a rag. Then she sat down to sew.

The bear returned home.

"What is the matter with your finger?" it asked.

"Nothing much. I was cutting some noodles and cut my finger too."

"Let me have a look."

"No, it might hurt!"

"I said: show me!" The bear tore the bandage off and saw — a gold finger.

"So you did go into the third cupboard after all!" it roared, killed the girl with its sharp teeth and threw her into the third cupboard behind the tubs. Once more the bear was alone.

Some time later the hairy, furry bear said to the cat with gold claws, "Cat with gold claws, find me a bride!"

"Very well then."

Cat gold claws went off to find one. Again it climbed the cottage fence, jumped from the fence into the apple tree and from the apple tree into the cabbages. The second daughter saw it.

"Father, father, a cat with gold claws is running about in our garden!"

"Catch it then!"

The girl ran out of the cottage. The cat jumped over the fence — the girl jumped over the fence; the cat ran along the path — the girl ran along the path; the cat leapt across the brook — the girl leapt across the brook; the cat went into the forest — the girl went into the forest; the cat entered into the cottage — the girl entered into the cottage.

The bear again was rubbing its paws with glee. "What a fine housekeeper you've brought me, my gold claw cat! Now you, good woman, look after us and feed us well and I will always bring you wood. Here is a set of keys. You can go into this cupboard and that one too, but if you open the third cupboard, I will kill you."

The next day the bear and the cat went for some wood. The girl went to the first cupboard, and found bread. She opened the second cupboard and found meat, honey and dripping; but what was in the third? She opened it too and found five tubs inside. Taking off the lid of the first tub, she dipped her finger into it and it turned gold. The frightened girl quickly locked the cupboard and bandaged her finger with a rag.

The bear came in and said:

"What is the matter with your finger?"

"I was cutting the grass and my finger got in the way."

"Show me!"

"No, it hurts too much."

The bear tore the bandage off and saw — a gold finger. Without further ado he bit her to death and threw her body into the third cupboard behind the tubs. Once more he was a widower.

The hairy, furry bear felt sad and lonely, so one day he said to the gold claw cat, "Gold claw cat, please find me a bride!"

"No I won't, for you bite to death every bride I find you!"

"I won't do it again, I'll be kind to her."

So cat gold claws went off again to find a bride. It climbed the cottage fence, jumped from the fence into the apple tree, from the apple tree into the cabbages. The youngest daughter saw it.

"Father, father, a cat with gold claws is running about in our garden!"

"Go and catch it!"

The girl ran out after the cat. The cat over the fence — the girl over the fence; the cat along the path — the girl along the path; the cat across the brook — the girl across the brook; the cat into the forest — the girl into the forest; the cat inside the cottage, the girl inside the cottage.

THE BRIDES OF THE BEAR

The bear was happy again. "You have brought me a fine wife, cat gold claws! Now, housekeeper, look after me and feed me well, and I will bring you plenty of wood in return. Here is a set of keys. You can open the first cupboard and the second one, but if you go into the third, I will kill you."

The next day the bear went to chop wood, but cat gold claws stayed behind. The girl went to the first cupboard and found some bread. She went to the second cupboard and found meat, dripping and honey. When she unlocked the third cupboard, she saw five tubs standing inside. As soon as she had taken the lid off the first, cat gold claws ran to her side and said, "Don't dip your finger into it, put a stick in it instead!"

The girl found a stick and dipped it into the first tub; it turned to gold. She dipped it into the second tub and it turned silver. When she dipped it into the third tub, it turned to lead. In the fourth tub it grew green, for it was filled with water of life, and in the fifth it shrivelled and died, for that tub was filled with dead water. The maiden then peeped behind the tubs.

"Alas, my poor dead sisters lie here, killed by the bear!"

The girl sprinkled the dead water over her eldest sister, and the fatal bite on her neck healed. She then sprinkled the water of life over her, and brought her sister back to life.

"Don't worry, sister, I will save you!"

When the bear came home, the girl was making pancakes.

"How did you get on today, my woman?"

"Very well. I looked at everything and found everything."

"Did you go into the third cupboard?"

"Of course not! You forbade me to do so."

"That is good. Now give me my dinner!"

"I will, but first take a basket of pancakes to my parents. It is my mother's birthday."

"Give me the basket then!"

The girl handed it over, but it was not only filled with pancakes. Her eldest sister sat inside and the pancakes were on top.

"You're not to eat those pancakes! I'll climb on the roof and watch that you don't."

The bear took the basket and went. He walked and walked, but the basket was very heavy.

"I think I'll put it down, have a rest and eat a few."

The voice of the eldest sister cried from the basket:

"Don't put the basket down, don't rest and don't eat any of the pancakes! I am standing on the roof and can see everything."

"What a sharp pair of eyes my wife must have to see all from so far away."

The bear walked on.

He reached the edge of the village and was met by a pack of angry dogs. The bear threw the basket to the ground and pelted back into the forest. The eldest sister crawled out of the basket and ran home.

The next day the girl sprinkled the dead water and the water of life over her elder sister, then sat her in a basket and covered her with potato cakes.

The bear returned home.

"Give me my dinner, wife."

"I will, but first take this basket of potato cakes to my parents. It is my father's birthday."

"All right then. Give me the basket."

"Don't you eat those potato cakes! I'll climb up on the roof and watch that you don't."

The bear put the basket on his back and went. He walked on and on, but the basket was very heavy.

"So what! I'll put the basket down, take a rest and eat a few potato cakes."

The second sister cried out from inside the basket, "Don't put the basket down, don't rest and don't eat any of the potato cakes! I am standing on the roof and can see everything!"

"Good gracious! What a sharp pair of eyes my wife must have! She sees all from such a distance."

And the bear walked on.

When he reached the village, the pack of dogs jumped on him. The bear dropped the basket and pelted back into the woods. The second sister crawled out of the basket and ran home.

When the next day the bear returned home, his wife was baking cakes.

"You are to take a basketful of these cakes to my parents. It is my brother's birthday. But you're not to eat any! I will climb onto the roof and see that you don't."

But the youngest sister did not climb up on the roof.

She placed a barrel there instead, with a broom; she wrapped her cloak round the barrel and tied her scarf to the broom. Then the girl crawled into the basket and covered herself with the cakes. The bear took the basket and set off. And he found the basket very heavy.

"So what! I'll put it down a while, take a rest and eat a few."

The youngest sister cried out of the basket, "Don't put the basket down, don't rest and don't eat the cakes! I am standing on the roof and I can see everything."

"What a pair of eyes! She sees all and from so far away."

The bear walked on.

At the edge of the village the dogs jumped on him again and he dropped the basket and pelted away.

The youngest sister jumped out of the basket and ran home.

When the bear returned home, he noticed that his wife was still standing on the roof.

"You can get down again now. I've taken the basket and am now back home."

The girl did not move and said not a word. The bear grew very cross; he shook the cottage hard and the barrel fell off.

"Wait a minute, woman, you will kill yourself," cried the bear and spread out his paws in an effort to catch her.

The barrel fell right on top of his head, the broom right on top of his nose and that was the end of our hairy, furry bear.

Nobody could find out what became of cat gold claw. Perhaps it still lives in the cottage, guarding the cupboard with the five tubs.

HOW THE BARON
CAME TO KNOW NECESSITY

It is said that in times of real necessity the devil would eat even cockroaches. I will tell you about a baron who, from sheer necessity, found himself pulling a sleigh in the place of his horse.

It happened one wintry day when a poor peasant was sawing logs in the forest. His clothes were thin and worn, instead of shoes there was straw tied round his feet and yet he sawed and sawed till steam came from his body.

A baron from a neighbouring estate passed by in his sleigh and he said:

"Good health to you, peasant! Why are you sawing wood when it is so cold and frosty?"

"Good health to you too, sir," said the peasant. "I am sawing wood from sheer necessity."

"From necessity?" asked the puzzled baron, turning to his coachman. "What is this necessity?"

The coachman shrugged his shoulders:

"I have no idea, master. I have never seen it, never heard of it."

The baron asked the peasant:

"Tell me, friend, what is 'necessity'? I have never seen it, never heard of it."

The peasant was annoyed that the wealthy baron was asking such silly questions, so he answered. "Run, sir, deep into the forest in that direction and necessity herself will find you."

The baron ran into the forest, his coachman with him.

They fell up to their knees into deep snowdrifts and grew tired and out of breath, but they did not meet necessity.

The baron said to the coachman:

"It is no good. It looks as if we will never meet 'necessity'. We had better return to the sledge."

They plodded back to the road.

In the meantime the peasant unharnessed the horses from the sledge and led them home. The sledge was left on the road. When the baron and the coachman stopped in front of the sledge, they stood aghast.

"What can we do?" said the baron. "We are not going to leave a perfectly good sledge behind. We will harness ourselves and pull it back into the village. There we can hire some horses and drive home."

The baron and his coachman then tied themselves to the sledge and started off. They pulled and pulled, until their legs were tired and as heavy as lead, until at last they reached the village.

Quite naturally people gathered round them, wondering why a baron and his coach-man had harnessed themselves to a sledge.

"Why?" shouted the baron angrily.

"From sheer necessity, sheer necessity, I tell you!"

And that is how the baron came face to face with necessity and all it cost him was three horses.

THE FLYING SHIP

All this happened a long time ago. Believe it or not, it is absolutely true.

One farmer had three sons: two clever ones, and one stupid one, whose name was Vanja. The clever pair had a great life, spending their time eating and drinking while Vanja did all the work.

The Czar of that kingdom announced one day that he would give his daughter to the man who came to fetch her in a flying ship, which would fly on its own in the air. The clever brothers decided to go to see the Czar's daughter, hoping they would find the flying ship on their way. Their mother baked them a big batch of buns and cakes and off they went. On their journey they met an old man.

"Please, young men, give an old beggar a morsel of food. I have not eaten a single mouthful for two days now."

"We too have nothing to eat," they said curtly.

"Of course you have. What is in your bundles?"

"We've been collecting fir cones."

The old man smiled sadly and walked on.

A little later, when the youths wanted to eat, they found only fir cones inside their bundles! So they turned round and went back home.

Vanja then set off to try his luck. His mother did not bother to bake him a batch of buns and cakes, but gave him only hard crusts to put in his bundle. Why should she bother with such a dimwit!

Vanja walked on and on, then he too met the old man.

"Please, young man, give an old beggar a morsel of food. I have not eaten a single mouthful for three days now."

"I would give you some gladly, grandfather, but all I have are hard crusts," Vanja replied.

"That does not matter. Even a hard crust is tasty, when one is truly hungry."

Vanja then untied his bundle and could hardly believe his eyes. It was full of fresh cakes and buns. When they had both eaten as much as they could, the old man asked, "Where exactly are you going, Vanja?"

"The Czar of our kingdom announced that he would give his daughter to the man who would come to fetch her in a flying ship. I am going to try my luck."

"Where is your flying ship?"

"I haven't one."

"In that case I will give you some advice," said the old man. "When you come to the wood, hit the first tree with your stick, then quickly lie flat on the ground, face downwards.

The ship will be built all on its own. Afterwards fly straight to the Czar's palace and give everyone whom you meet on the way a ride to. Do you understand?"

Vanja nodded his head and the old man disappeared.

Vanja walked to the wood, hit the first tree with his stick and fell face downwards flat on the ground.

Then there was the noise of scraping, banging, chopping and sawing and in a trice a beautiful flying ship stood right in front of Vanja. He climbed inside and flew towards the palace.

He flew on and on, till he saw a man hopping along the path on one leg, because his other was tied to his ear.

"Why don't you untie your leg?" Vanja cried out to him.

"If I untied it and used both feet, I would cross half the world with just one leap."

"In that case climb in and fly with me, Longlegs!"

They flew on, till they saw a man on the road with a gun. He was aiming into nothing.

"What are you aiming at, friend?" Vanja called out.

"I want to shoot a sparrow which is flying on the other side of the world. My eyes are that sharp."

"Climb in and fly with us, Sharpeyes!"

They flew on, till they saw a man with his ear glued to the ground.

"What are you listening to, friend?" wondered Vanja.

"I am listening to the grass growing, so acute is my hearing."

"Climb in and fly with us, Keenears!"

They flew on, till they saw a man with a cart filled with bread, hurrying somewhere.

"Why are you in such a hurry?" Vanja asked.

"I am looking for something to eat," the man replied.

"But you have a whole cartful of bread."

"That's nothing! I'd eat in one session twenty such carts and the horses as well."

"Climb in and fly with us, Guzzler, but don't eat us up too!" said Vanja laughingly and they flew on.

A little later they saw a man standing by a pond.

"Why are you standing there, my friend?"

"I have a terrible thirst!"

"Drink some of the pond water then!"

"That would be just like a sip to me. I need to drink a whole ocean, but there the water is salty and I don't like that."

"Climb in and fly with us, Swiller!"

They flew on, till they saw a man whose beret was stuffed in his mouth.

"Surely you don't want to eat your own beret!" laughed Vanja.

"Of course not! I just try to block my mouth. My breath is so icy that when I breathe everything round me freezes."

"Climb in and fly with us, Blast-ice!" Vanja offered, and they flew on till they were very nearly at the palace. Then they saw a man with a drum on his belly.

"Hey, Drummer, beat your drum!"

"I can't do that. As soon as I beat the drum, soldiers start marching from my drum and as long as I keep on playing, they keep on marching."

"Climb in and fly with us, Drummer!"

A few minutes later they flew down into the palace courtyard. The Czar happened to be looking out of the palace window and was astonished to see that a hopeful bridegroom really managed to fly to him in a flying ship. But he was not very keen, however, to give his daughter to stupid Vanja, nor did he like his strange looking companions. He said to himself, "I'll set you such tasks, hopeful bridegroom, that you'll lose your appetite for marriage."

Though the Czar said these words almost silently, Keenears heard them and told his companions the Czar was up to something. The Czar said to them, "You must be terribly hungry and thirsty after such a journey, so I've had a meal prepared for you. But you must eat and drink everything. Otherwise Vanja will not get my daughter."

A dozen roast calves and cakes from a dozen ovens were placed before them, with forty huge barrels of wine. But the Czar did not win! Guzzler and Swiller ate and drank with relish and soon there was no trace of food or drink left. The others never had even a cake, or a single sip.

"So you managed it all," grumbled the Czar. "Now that you have had your fill, you can bring me the golden apple which grows on the apple tree one thousand miles from here. Mind you, I want it by nightfall."

This was a simple task for Longlegs! He untied his leg and with a single leap was a thousand miles away, right underneath the apple tree with the golden apples. As he had plenty of time left, he slumped under the tree and fell fast asleep. He slept on and on until it was nearly evening and he was still asleep.

"I wonder what has happened to Longlegs?" Vanja said worriedly.

"Don't worry," Sharpeyes assured him. He focused his eyes into the distance and immediately found Longlegs asleep under the tree. Taking his rifle he aimed and shot down an apple from the tree. It fell right on the tip of Longleg's nose! He woke, rubbed his eyes, picked up the golden apple and with one step was back in the palace.

"I am not getting anywhere with them," the Czar muttered to himself, when Vanja handed him the golden apple. "I'll have them all put into a red hot oven, let them roast alive!"

Keenears heard it all and Blast-ice wasted no time in taking the beret out of his mouth. The moment he blew into the red hot oven, the fire went out and it was freezing instead. In fact they had to ask to be let out, so they would not all freeze to death.

Now the Czar really did not know what to do.

"I will just have to pretend to give my daughter to Vanja. But as they get into the flying ship, I will send my soldiers after him and they will take my daughter from him."

Once again Keenears heard everything and told Drummer to be at the ready with his drum.

When the Czar's soldiers charged Vanja, so they could take the princess from him, Drummer started to beat his drum and he kept on beating and beating it and soldier after soldier kept on marching out — one regiment after another. These regiments chased away the Czar's soldiers, arrested the Czar and his councillors, and because a Czardom cannot stay without a Czar, they made simple Vanja their new Czar.

The seven strange companions became his loyal councillors. They lived happily and in prosperity and so did all their Czardom.

THE UNHAPPY
ARMLESSA

In a certain town there once lived a wealthy merchant who had two children, a boy and a girl. When the merchant was dying, he said to his son, "Dearest son, live with your sister in harmony, peace and love. Live honestly and do not cheat people. When the time comes for you to marry, do not choose a bride from this town."

After their father's death, the brother and sister lived together as harmoniously as two doves. Each morning, as the brother left home for the shop, he would say, "Goodbye, my dearest sister!" And each evening, as he returned, "How are you, my dearest sister?" So it went on for three years and three days.

Then the brother said, "Dearest sister, the time has come for me to marry. I have chosen a bride from this town."

The sister was most distressed. "Please, dearest brother, do not marry a bride from this town. Remember what your father told you with his last breath."

But the brother paid no heed and married the bride from his town. She was beautiful to look at, but her heart was as cold as ice. From the moment she realized that the sister was not in favour of the marriage, she decided to have her revenge.

The brother carried on as before. Each morning, as he left home for the shop, he would say, "Goodbye, dearest sister!" And each evening, as he returned, "How are you, my dearest sister?"

The brother had a dog and he was very fond of it. One day his wife killed the dog and when he returned from work, she said to him, "You have a cruel sister, for she has killed your dog!"

The brother was most upset, but he said nothing and forgave his sister.

The brother also owned a horse, which he loved to ride. One day his wicked wife killed the horse too. When her husband returned home in the evening, she said, "You have an evil sister, for she has killed your horse!"

The brother was even more upset, but he still said nothing and forgave his sister.

Some time later the wife gave birth to a baby, a beautiful, rosy cheeked baby. One day she took the child and killed it. When the husband returned in the evening she sobbed, "Alas, husband! Your dreadful, wicked sister has now killed our baby!"

The brother shed bitter tears and was furious with his sister. Taking an axe, he led her deep into the forest. There he made her undress completely and chopped off her arms at her elbows. He left her to be bitten to death by mosquitoes and flies, or devoured by wild beasts. The sister swore and begged that she was innocent, but he did not believe her.

It so happened that a young Czar rode to hunt in that forest. He came to the very spot, where the unhappy Armlessa was hiding. When he saw something move in the bushes, he pointed his gun and cried, "Who is in the bushes? Is it a human being, is it a wild beast, or some evil magic?"

Armlessa replied, "Please do not shoot me, Czar! I am a human being."

When the Czar heard the melodious voice, he said, "Come on out! If you are older than I, you will be my mother; if you are younger than I, you will be my dear wife."

Armlessa cried out, "I can't come out, for I have not even a petticoat!"

The young Czar passed her his cloak and Armlessa came out of the bushes. And she became the Czar's wife.

For a short time they lived together in happiness and contentment, but then the young Czar had to leave to go to war. A few weeks after he left, a son was born to Armlessa, as handsome as the sun. The young Czar's father was delighted and wrote a letter straight away to his son with the news. It was given to the fastest messenger.

The messenger saddled his horse and rode like the wind through the deep forests under the high skies. In the late evening he came to the town where Armlessa's brother and his wicked wife were living. Because it was already dark, the messenger asked the merchant if he could stay overnight.

"Where are you from and where are you going?" asked the wife after supper.

The messenger told them that he was taking a letter to the young Czar. And he related how the young Czar married his Armlessa and what a beautiful baby they had.

The nasty, shrewd sister-in-law straight away realized what was what, that Armlessa was her husband's sister. She prepared a bath for the messenger and when he was safely in it, she took from his pocket the letter from the old Czar and placed another in its place. She wrote, "Your wife has given birth to a monster, with the body of a cat, legs of a goat, head and face of a monkey."

The Czar was sadly surprised when he read this letter, but he said nothing and wrote back to say that nothing should be done with the mother or the baby till he returned.

The speedy messenger rode again through deep forests under high skies, till by the late evening he arrived at the house of the young merchant again. He decided to spend another night there. The wicked wife prepared a bath for the messenger and while he was in it, she took the letter from the young Czar out of his pocket and placed another in its place. She wrote, "Kill the mother and the child!"

When the old Czar read this, he had such a terrible shock he fell to the floor and never rose again. Everyone in the castle was sorry for the mother and the baby, but no one dared disobey the command of their Czar. So a gamekeeper was sent into the forest with Armlessa and the baby, with instructions to leave them there. If it was the will of God, then the wild beasts would eat them both.

The poor unfortunate Armlessa held the baby with her stumps, which was all that remained of her arms, and walked and walked wherever her feet took her. The hot sun burned her, the cold rain chilled her, but she kept on walking, till she met an old man. "Where are you going, Armlessa?" he asked.

"Alas, grandfather, I care not where I go. The sun is burning me, the rain chills me, but I walk on and on."

The old man said, "What are you carrying, Armlessa?"

"It is my baby, grandfather. But my son is not like others. When I lay him by horses, they don't neigh; when I lay him by cows, they don't moo; when I lay him by sheep, they don't stamp their hooves."

"Oh, Armlessa," said the old man. "Just look how your son keeps opening his mouth! Give him a drink, for he is thirsty!"

Armlessa bent over a nearby brook, so the baby could have a drink. But as she leant over, the child slipped from the stumps and began floating away with the current.

Armlessa cried bitterly over her unhappy life. How helpless she felt, when with only stumps for her arms she could not save her child from drowning! But the old man spoke to her encouragingly:

"Try, Armlessa, try and pull your baby out of the water! Go on, don't be afraid, try!"

Armlessa immersed what remained of her arms into the water, and lo and behold! The moment they were under, the rest of her arms and her hands grew again and were as before. Quickly she snatched her baby out of the current and turned to thank the old man. But he was gone. Suddenly she knew, deep in her heart, that the old man was no other than her late father.

Armlessa plodded on and on, till she came to the town where her brother and her evil sister-in-law lived. She knocked on their door, asking for a bed for the night. The merchant asked her in, not realizing she was his own sister. Even his wife did not recognize her. How could they, when she had both her arms and hands now.

It so happened that this very night the young Czar was returning home. As he still had a fair way to go to his palace, he too stopped at the merchant's house for the night. After all, the house was right at the edge of the town. They all met at the dinner table: brother with his sister, husband with his wife, father with his baby son — but they did not know about each other. Not even the Czar recognized Armlessa with both her arms.

Armlessa cried and cried. Bitter tears rolled down her cheeks and everyone asked her why she was weeping so.

"It is of no importance. I was thinking of a very sad story."

The Czar said, "Tell us this story and stop crying! A story is, after all, just a story; it pours from the mouth and flies away with the wind."

Armlessa replied:

"I will tell you the story, if you all promise not to interrupt."

They all gave their word, so Armlessa began, "In a certain Czardom there once lived a merchant, who had a son and a daughter. When this merchant was on his death bed, he said to his son, 'Dearest son, live with your sister in harmony, peace and love. When the time comes for you to marry, do not choose a bride from our town.' The father died and the son paid no attention to his words, but married a girl from his town. His bride was lovely on the outside, but had a heart as cold as ice. She was determined to destroy her husband's sister. He had a dog, whom he loved very much. The bride killed the dog and told her husband that this was the work of his own sister."

"That's a lie, I didn't kill the dog! Nor the horse, nor the baby!" cried the merchant's wife.

So the real truth leaked out as surely as oil floats to the surface of running water.

The enraged brother turned on his wicked wife and chased her into the forest, so wild beasts could tear her to pieces as she justly deserved. Then he begged his sister to forgive him, asking her to try and forget how he had wronged her.

The young Czar was overjoyed, for he was reunited with his dearest wife and his bonny baby, as lovely as the sun.

They all rode back to the palace and lived together for the rest of their lives in harmony, peace and love.

HOW THE FOX
AND THE WOLF CAUGHT
THEIR FISH

This story is about a different wolf and a different fox from those I have already told you about. This pair had such bushy tails, which reached right down to the ground. But this wolf too was a fool above fools, and the fox, to tell the truth, was smarter than all the Czar's council.

It all began like this:

There was an old man and an old woman. One winter's day the old man said, "Make some dumplings, granny. I am off to the pond to catch some fish. We shall eat well today."

Whilst the old woman made the dough, the old man harnessed the sleigh and went fishing.

His catch was large and soon he was merrily returning home. On his way back he saw our clever fox stretched on the ground. It lay there, quite still.

"It must have frozen to death," the old man said to himself. "I'll take it home, it will make a fur coat for my wife."

He picked up the fox and threw it into the sleigh. But the fox was far from dead — it was only pretending. The moment the old man turned his back and drove off, the fox raised its head, looked around carefully, then slowly and quietly began to throw fish after fish off the sleigh. When the very last fish was on the path, the fox jumped off, too.

The old man came home and said to his wife:

"Here I am, granny, with a sleigh full of fish and a fox fur and all!"

Granny looked, but found nothing; there was no fox, nor a single fish.

By then the artful fox had gathered all the fish strewn on the path and was having a real feast. It gulped fish after fish, smacking its lips with satisfaction.

A wolf ran by, "Good-day, foxie!"

"Good-day, wolf!"

"What are you eating, foxie?" asked the wolf.

"Can't you see? Fish, of course!"

"Give me a little fish too!"

"Why should I? Catch some yourself!"

"But I don't know how to fish."

"It is ever so easy, wolfie. Run to the pond over there, cut a hole in the ice, put your tail into it and you'll see, the fish will hook themselves onto it all on their own."

The wolf thanked the fox nicely and followed its advice. It cut a hole through the ice, pushed its tail into it and waited for the fish to come. It sat and sat the whole night long and as there was a sharp frost, the tail froze solid into the ice.

The wolf tried to pull its tail out. It pulled and pulled, but the tail would not budge.

(178) 179   HOW THE FOX AND THE WOLF
CAUGHT THEIR FISH

"My tail is so weighed with fish, I can't even pull it out," it thought happily and carried on fishing.

In the morning the village women came to the pond to fetch water. When they saw the wolf they began to shout:

"A wolf, a wolf! Thrash it, hit it!"

The wolf was terrified and tried to run away. But, oh dear, it was just impossible. The tail was frozen solid. The women picked up whatever was handy — a stick, a pail, a stone — and they set upon the wolf. The poor beast had quite a thrashing and it could just not get away; it was well and truly stuck. Then at last the wolf tugged so hard that it freed itself and it ran and ran as if all the women were hot on its heels.

But the wolf's tail stayed frozen in the ice. So it happened that from that day, yet another silly wolf roamed the woods without its tail.

PETER OF THE GOLDEN KEYS

Far, far away lies the French kingdom, where once upon a time a French count lived, who had a son named Peter. This son excelled so much in bravery and strength that there was no one who could match him. Because of this Peter said to his father one day, "Dear father, I must leave you and travel round the world, so I can meet new people and so I can take part in tournaments in foreign lands. I hope that by winning the fights with their knights and heroes I will bring fame and glory to our race."

When Peter bade his father and mother goodbye, they gave him three gold rings as a keepsake, to remind him never to forget them and never to bring shame upon them.

Peter rode from the kingdom, further and further, till he reached the Neapolitan Czardom and came to the Czar's court. The Neapolitan Czar was curious to know who this stranger was, so he asked Peter, "Tell me, young man, what is your birth and what do you seek here?"

Peter replied, "My name is Peter, gracious Czar, but I am not of noble birth. I have ridden from the French kingdom to see the world, meet new people and to fight in foreign tournaments, for I have beaten all the knights in my own country."

The Neapolitan Czar then said, "You will be pleased to hear, Peter, that we are holding a grand tournament right here in my court in a week's time. All the gallant knights and noblemen will gather and you will have the chance to prove your strength and bravery."

Eleven Neapolitan knights entered the tournament; Peter was the twelfth. He knocked them all down and beat them all, and was pronounced the winner of the tournament.

The Neapolitan Czar had a daughter Magilena, who was charming and beautiful. When Peter saw her watching the fight from the royal enclosure, he fell in love with her and secretly made up his mind that one day he would make her his wife. As the lovely Magilena presented him with a garland of flowers at the end of the tournament, Peter gazed deeply into her eyes and placed on her finger one of the three rings his parents had given him. Magilena blushed and lowered her eyes, for she too liked the gallant, handsome youth.

A week later another tournament was held. This time twenty-three gallant Neapolitan knights took part; Peter was the twenty-fourth. Once again he beat them all. When the beautiful Magilena gave him the garland of flowers for the second time, he placed upon her finger the second ring his parents had given him.

By then everyone in the Neapolitan Czardom was talking about the gallant knight Peter. When the third tournament was held, fifty-nine knights took part; Peter was the sixtieth one. All the brave men in the Czardom wanted to try to match their strength against him. But Peter beat them all and was the outright winner.

Even the Neapolitan Czar was most impressed and said, "I have seen many things in my life, but never such gallantry and strength. As you are not of noble birth, I promote you to the rank of knighthood and give you two golden keys as your crest. Respect your crest and bring it only fame and honour! And, as a further reward, I will grant you one wish."

Peter then knelt before the Czar and said:

"Gracious Czar, please do not be annoyed, for I have lied to you. I am not of common birth, for my father is a French count. And I have only one wish, and that is for you to give me your lovely daughter Magilena to be my wife."

The Neapolitan Czar thought awhile. He knew the French count well, he happened to be a very dear friend, so he had no objections to his son marrying the beautiful Magilena. Therefore he said, "My dear young knight, providing my daughter wishes to marry you, I give you my permission and my word."

Peter was overjoyed and straight away walked over to Magilena and placed the third ring upon her finger. Once again the lovely maiden blushed deeply and lowered her eyes, but kept her hand in Peter's firm clasp.

The Neapolitan Czar could see clearly that his daughter had no objections against her bridegroom, so he started making the wedding arrangements. But Peter of the golden keys then said, "Gracious Czar! I left my house to bring honour and fame to my family. But I want my father's blessing for this marriage. I must return home before we can hold the wedding."

The Czar praised Peter for his thoughtfulness, but Magilena said, "I have promised never to be willingly parted from my dearest Peter. Please, father, let me go with him to the French kingdom, so his parents can meet me."

The Neapolitan Czar and the Czarina were unhappy to hear their daughter's wish, but in the end they agreed. Soon, Peter of the golden keys and his beautiful Magilena set off to the French kingdom with a whole retinue of servants.

They rode on and on, till they came to a dense forest. The path zig-zagged all over the place, till it was lost altogether in a thicket. As Peter and Magilena were right in the rear, they did not know in which direction to go and lost their way completely.

They called the others in vain; no one answered them. They were alone in the forest. Peter tried to cheer up Magilena, "Don't worry that we are lost. I will find the right path again and we shall reach the French kingdom. We must make for the sea shore."

They rode on and truly, some time later, they came to the sea shore. They slid from their saddles, and as Magilena was terribly tired, she fell asleep. Peter gazed at her, taking in her beauty. As he looked, he noticed a tiny satin bag tied to Magilena's throat. He untied it and found inside the three rings he had given her. Just as he placed the rings back in the bag, a large, greedy bird flew down, scooped the red bag with its beak and flew off again.

Peter ran after the bird. He ran and ran, throwing stones after it, till one of them hit the bird. By then it was flying over the sea and dropped the satin bag on a steep rock not too far from the shore.

Peter walked along the beach, wondering how he could get it. As it happened, luck was with him, for he found a small boat hidden in the reeds. Soon he was paddling towards the rock. Just when he was right by it, a fierce gale blew up and tossed the little boat far into the open sea. Peter was frightened and began to weep, thinking he would never see his Magilena again; all this time his boat drifted further and further out to sea. A Moorish pirate ship sailed by and as the pirates saw Peter of the golden keys in his little boat, they stopped and pulled him on deck.

When the captain of the ship saw the handsome youth dressed in his smart, expensive clothes, he liked him very much and decided to give Peter to the Moor-King himself.

They sailed on and on till the ship reached Alexandria, the Moorish capital. Peter was then given to the Moor-King.

The Moor-King said that first Peter must learn Moorish customs and morals. As Peter proved an excellent and an eager pupil, he gained the respect of everyone in the Moor kingdom.

But what was happening to poor Magilena?

When she awoke, she was most surprised to see her red satin bag had gone. But she was startled and grieved when she could not find her beloved. She waited and waited till morning, but it was no use.

As she did not know what to do, Magilena saddled her horse and rode on along the sea shore. Peter's horse trotted close behind her, its head sadly bowed. They rode on and on, till they came to a road. This road led to Rome and an inn was built at the roadside.

Magilena went inside, sold both the horses and her beautiful clothes. Then she dressed herself in the robe of a nun and walked on, till she came to the sea. A ship happened to be leaving the dock, so Magilena stepped on deck and sailed to St. Peter's island. And there she stayed, for she said to herself, "I shall settle here, and build a chapel and a hospital for the sick in memory of my unfortunate Peter of the golden keys."

This is exactly what she did. The chapel and the hospital were built and soon people from far and wide were talking about them and about the virtuous life of the lovely Magilena. She lived in this manner for three long years.

One day some fishermen brought a huge fish to Magilena. When they cut it open, they found the red satin bag with the three gold rings in its stomach. Magilena realized that these were the same rings Peter of the golden keys had given her and took this as the final proof that Peter had definitely drowned. She cried bitterly in her unhappiness, but tied the red satin bag round her neck once more.

Peter spent these three years at the Moorish court and he was treated well. But all the time he thought of his Magilena and wondered how he could get out of his enslavement. One day he said to the Moor-King, "As I have served you faithfully these past three years, I beg of you now to fulfil my only wish. Please let me visit my father, the French count."

The Moor-King would not hear of it at first, but when Peter kept on asking and begging, he agreed and said, "Peter of the golden keys, I will let you go for three months. After that time you must return and go on serving me faithfully."

Peter of the golden keys then went to the port, took ten sacks of gold from the Moor-King's safe, sprinkled salt on top and waited for a ship to take him to the French kingdom.

When an opportune ship came by, he took it. He was thrilled to think how easily he got out of his captivity and lived in hope that perhaps he would, after all, see his Magilena again. A week later they were still on the open sea, but not too far away from the French kingdom. By then they were at the end of their fresh water supply, so the captain issued an order to dock by a nearby island. Luckily, they found a fresh water spring there. While the crew were busy filling the tubs with the water, Peter strolled to a wood, sat in the soft moss and fell asleep.

When all the water holders were filled and back on ship, the captain wanted to sail on. But they could not find Peter. They called him in vain, they searched for him in vain. Eventually the captain decided that poor Peter must have drowned, and sailed away with his ship.

On the way the captain thought of looking into the sacks which Peter of the golden keys brought with him. When he saw salt on top, he concluded they were of no particular value and when they docked on the island of St. Peter, he gave the sacks to the hospital for the sick.

This of course was the very hospital built by the beautiful Magilena.

When Peter of the golden keys woke up and realized the ship had sailed away, leaving him behind, he was very worried and very sad, for he had no idea how to get away from the island. He could only hope that some passing ship may have to stop there for water and take him off too.

Some time later, fishermen, who were fishing near the island, noticed Peter lying on the beach. As he happened to be in a deep sleep, they took him for a dead man, but they put him in their boat and rowed him to St. Peter's island, so he could at least have a decent funeral.

The moment the beautiful Magilena saw him, she recognized her beloved. She began to weep bitterly and her hot tears fell on Peter's cheeks, waking him up. He stirred and opened his eyes. He was far from dead! How happy they both were!

Soon preparations for a huge wedding were in full swing. Many noble lords and noble ladies came from near and far, including the French count and countess and the Neapolitan Czar and Czarina. They were all happy and delighted to see how deeply and faithfully their children loved one another and how they conquered all the obstacles which fate had put between them.

IVAN AND
MICHAEL WATERS

An old man once lived in a certain village of a certain district in a certain Czardom. This old man had an unmarried daughter. As she was no longer young, she was very unhappy that she had never had any children. Who would look after her when she was really old?

One day the daughter went to get water with two pails. She drew some water with the left pail and had a little drink. Then she filled the right pail and had another sip. Forty hours later two sons were born from this water. They were handsome and as alike as two peas in a pod. As they came from water, they were christened Ivan Waters and Michael Waters.

The boys grew not with years, not with days, but with hours and minutes, as swiftly as the bread dough rises. When they were only six weeks old, they were big enough to go out into the world.

"Oh, my sons, why do you want to leave home when you are still so young? I have hardly had a chance to enjoy being with you, or to have pleasure from having you, and you are leaving me already."

Their mother, the old man's daughter, complained bitterly, but it was no use.

Ivan Waters and Michael Waters left home. They walked on and on, till they came to a cross-road, bearing two signs, "The one who takes the left path, will find riches," read the first. And the other, "Who takes the right path, will find death."

Michael Waters tossed a small stone on to the ground and it rolled on to the path which led to riches. Ivan Waters threw a stone too, and it rolled on the path of death. Ivan Waters said, "We must part, dear brother. You have to follow the path to riches and I, the path of death. I will give you my gold ring. If it grows black, I shall no longer be amongst the living."

Here is the story of Ivan Waters.

He walked on and on, till he reached a wide meadow, where there was an old inn. The inn-keeper said, "What misfortune brings you here? A terrible dragon rages here. You would not believe how many people he's devoured! And today it's the Czar's daughter's turn."

"What sort of a dragon is he?" asked Ivan.

"The most horrifying dragon, the three-headed Gobbler."

"When is he due to kill the Czar's daughter?"

"Today at noon. Look on that hilltop; the Czar's daughter awaits him with sobs and tears."

Ivan Waters remarked firmly, "I am off to kill that dragon."

And off he went.

IVAN

AND MICHAEL WATERS

When he had climbed the hill, he found the Czar's daughter, lovely Marja, dressed all in white, crying bitterly. Ivan Waters turned to her, "Why do you weep, lovely damsel?"

"Who wouldn't weep in my place, when at noon the dragon is coming to slay me. But what are you doing here? Hurry away. The dragon will be here shortly; he'll gobble me up and is not likely to spare you!"

"I am not afraid of the dragon, and you too must not be afraid! I'll sort him out! I'll just rest a while first to gain more strength. Wake me up when the dragon comes."

Ivan Waters sat on the ground, cushioned his head on Marja's lap and fell asleep. A few moments later a terrible gale sprang up; the trees swayed and hissed, and the thunder roared to mark the arrival of the terrible, dreaded dragon, three-headed Gobbler.

The young Czarina tried hard to wake Ivan, but he slept so soundly, he did not even flicker and eyelid.

Marja tried again and again, but alas in vain. He slept like the dead. The dragon was already landing on the ground, ready to attack the maiden. Marja was so grieved to think of her wasted young life; wasted only because Ivan Waters was so sound asleep, she could not wake him. Her eyes welled with tears and one hot tear fell upon Ivan's forehead and he woke up.

"Why are you burning me, Marja?"

As he spoke, he noticed the three-headed Gobbler. Jumping to his feet, he faced the monster bravely. He swung his sword and with one quick swipe cut off the first head, then the second and the third. Then he cut the dragon's body into pieces and hid the bones under a stone.

The lovely Marja thanked him tearfully and took him home to her father, the Czar. The father was so happy to see that Ivan Waters had truly slain the dragon and had saved the life of his daughter, that he straight away held a wedding for his lovely Marja and Ivan Waters.

Ivan Waters lived very happily with his Marja for quite some time and he kept telling himself. "That sign on the cross-roads must have been wrong."

One fine day Ivan Waters went to bathe in a lake near the palace. As soon as he neared the water, a small bird circled over his head. It was a silver bird with a golden tail, with diamond eyes and a heavenly voice. Ivan followed the bird, walking on and on, further and further, till he reached a small cottage built on stilts in the middle of a dense forest. He had never been in this forest. The bird perched upon the cottage roof. Just as Ivan prepared to catch the bird, the wind blew suddenly, the trees hissed, and Granny Jaga flew in, her skinny legs folded in a mortar. She used a pestle for an oar, and a broom to sweep away her traces.

"So you have come for the silver bird with the golden tail, diamond eyes and a heavenly voice," she croaked.

"That is so, granny."

"Come nearer then, so I can have a good look at you."

Ivan stepped nearer. Granny Jaga touched his shoulder with her broom and the poor youth turned to rock.

"Now I have avenged you, my poor departed son, my three-headed horrific dragon Gobbler!" Granny Jaga screeched wickedly.

Now we must tell the story about Michael Waters.

After Michael Waters had bidden his brother goodbye at the cross-roads, he walked on for quite some time, following his path. He was terribly hungry and thirsty and so desperately tired he stumbled over stones, but there seemed no end to the forest path. There was no town to be seen, not even a village, or a lonely dwelling. Michael said to himself, "This is a nasty path. I doubt it will lead me to riches! It seems more likely I will die of hunger and thirst."

No sooner had he spoken than an old man stood before him, saying, "You are hungry and thirsty, are you not, Michael Waters?"

"I certainly am," Michael agreed, wondering how the old man knew him.

"I have a crust of bread and a few sips of water in this cup. I shall share them with you, though I am as thirsty and as hungry as you are."

Michael answered, "Keep it for yourself, Grandfather. There is not enough for two and as I am younger than you, I should be stronger."

"I can see, my boy, that you have a good heart. Because of that I will give you this serviette. It is no ordinary serviette. You only need to say 'Open up, serviette, open!' — and you will see."

Michael took the serviette, but before he could thank the old man, he had disappeared. So he said, "Open up, serviette, open!"

As soon as he had uttered these words, the serviette spread itself upon the ground and there were many delicious dishes on it, many of which Michael had not even tasted before. So he ate and he drank till he could eat and drink no more, and continued his journey. He had only walked about a hundred paces when he came to an inn. As night was approaching, Michael decided to stop there for the night.

"You can sleep here, but I have no food left," said the inn-keeper.

"That does not matter, for I can provide my own food," Michael assured him with a smile and said, "Open up, serviette, open!"

The inn-keeper's eyes nearly popped out of his head, when he saw the napkin's tricks and he thought:

"I could certainly do with such a napkin! How my business would flourish!"

When Michael Waters was sound asleep over the stove, the inn-keeper crept to his side and changed the magic napkin for an ordinary one.

The next morning Michael Waters rose, spread the napkin upon the table, and called, "Open up, serviette, open!" but the napkin did not move.

"Your magic doesn't seem to work today," sneered the inn-keeper. Michael jumped up and left.

"This path is a bad one after all," he grumbled. "I think I will turn back home."

So he walked back. He walked on and on, till suddenly he came face to face with the old man who had given him the napkin the day before.

"Where are you going, Michael Waters? Not home, I hope!"

"I am going home. I seem to have no luck at all. The napkin you gave me yesterday does not work any more."

"Really?" wondered the grandfather. "I'll give you something else then."

The old man whistled softly and a ram ran to his side. The old man gave it to Michael. "Pay attention, for this is no ordinary ram. All you have to do is to say, 'Shake, ram, shake!' and you will see. I'll give you another piece of advice. Don't go back home!"

Then the old man disappeared.

Michael shook his head over such words, but said, "Shake, ram, shake!"

As soon as he had spoken, the ram shook itself and a gold rouble fell out of its woolly coat. Michael laughed happily, picked up the rouble, and, taking the ram, went forward again.

As night was approaching, he stopped at the very inn where he had spent the previous night.

"I'll give you a bed and a good supper, but only if you can pay for them," said the inn-keeper.

"I have plenty of money, that's no problem," laughed Michael and called to the ram: "Shake, ram, shake!"

The ram shook itself a couple of times and by then Michael had a fistful of gold roubles.

The inn-keeper wasted no time. He filled the table with food and drink, and as soon as Michael had his fill and had fallen fast asleep over the stove, he changed the magic ram for another ram, which he had in the pen.

The next morning Michael Waters left the inn and said to the ram, "Shake, ram, shake!"

The ram shook itself, but no gold coins fell to the ground.

Michael was furious and decided he would go home after all. And off he went. After some time he suddenly came face to face again with the old man. "Where are you going, Michael Waters? Not home, I hope!"

"Yes, I am," Michael answered firmly. "I've had enough. The ram you gave me yesterday does not give gold roubles any more."

"Is that so?" wondered the old man. "In that case I will help you just once again. Here is a bag, but it is no ordinary bag. When you say, 'Forty out of the bag!' you will see what happens. Then you say, 'Forty back in the bag!' And don't forget to call at that inn. Do you understand?"

The old man was gone. Michael took the bag and called, "Forty out of the bag!"

As soon as he had spoken, forty strong fellows jumped from the bag, sticks and all, and started to thrash Michael. Quickly he shouted: "Forty back in the bag!" but by then his back was already black and blue. Michael did not mind that, however. Merrily he strode to the inn and said to the inn-keeper, "I've come for the night again. I have this bag with me. Can I leave it somewhere safe?"

"What do you want with such an old, worn-out bag? Throw it on the floor by the stove."

"I can't do that, for it is no ordinary bag. You should see what it can do! All one has to say is, 'Forty out of the bag!'"

The inn-keeper eyed the bag greedily and the moment Michael was asleep, he grabbed the bag and said: "Forty out of the bag!"

As soon as he had spoken, the forty strong fellows armed with sticks jumped from the bag and gave the inn-keeper such a thrashing! He cried and pleaded for help, till Michael Waters woke up.

"Please send these fellows away, Michael Waters, before my soul leaves my body."

"Will you then give me back my magic napkin?"

"I don't know anything about such a napkin," mumbled the inn-keeper.

"In that case you send them away!"

"Please, Michael Waters, help me! I'll give you back your napkin," promised the inn-keeper.

"And the ram too?"

"And the ram too!"

"Promise you won't cheat people in the future?"

"I promise. I really won't! But please help me!"

Michael Waters then called, "Forty back in the bag!" and the strong fellows jumped back into the bag, sticks and all.

The inn-keeper hastily returned the napkin and the ram to Michael.

Michael walked on, till he came to a large town. He settled there, opened a shop and soon became wealthy and respected throughout the district.

One day the old man, who had given him the napkin, the ram and the bag, called on Michael unexpectedly. "Well, Michael Waters, did the path lead to riches?"

"It certainly did, Grandfather. I don't know how to repay you."

"You don't have to repay me, but give me back the napkin, the ram and the bag. You don't need them any more, so they can now serve someone else."

Michael returned the magic gifts to the old man, bade him goodbye and wished him a happy journey, and good luck.

"I too wish you a happy journey and luck!" said the old man and disappeared.

"I wonder why he said that?" wondered Michael. "I am not going anywhere."

Then he glanced at the ring his brother had given him, and he saw that it had turned black. Realizing that Ivan must be in terrible trouble, he told his assistant to look after the shop and hurried to the cross-roads, and then along the path which led to death.

Michael Waters later arrived in the Czar's palace, where Marja greeted him joyfully. "Where have you been all this time, dearest Ivan? I was beginning to fear something had happened to you."

(194) 195   IVAN
             AND MICHAEL WATERS

Michael then knew that she took him for his brother Ivan, for they were identical, and he burst into bitter tears.

"What is the matter, dearest, who has harmed you that you are so sad you have not even kissed me yet?" asked the lovely Marja. But Michael Waters said nothing and rode swiftly away.

He came to a lake near the Czar's palace, where a silver bird circled above his head — a silver bird with a golden beak and eyes of diamonds. Michael followed the bird and lost his way in the dense forest, and found himself by the cottage on stilts. The bird perched on its roof.

Michael Waters was just about to catch the bird, when the wind blew up fiercely, hissing and moaning through the trees. Granny Jaga flew in as from nowhere, her skinny legs in a mortar. The mother of the dragon Gobbler used a pestle for an oar, sweeping away her traces with a broom.

"Did you come for the silver bird with the golden beak and diamond eyes?" she asked slyly.

"Yes, Granny."

"Come nearer then, so I can have a good look at you."

Michael stepped closer and the old hag raised her broomstick ready to strike. But Michael was the faster of the two. He gripped her wrist and tore the handle from her hand and hit her with it. Then Granny Jaga turned to stone.

Michael now realized what awful fate had befallen his brother Ivan: Granny Jaga had turned him to stone, just as she had wanted to do to him. Looking round, he noticed the second rock.

"I wonder if that could be my brother," he mused, and threw the broomstick at the rock. It turned into Ivan!

"Where have you come from, dear brother?" asked the bewildered Ivan. "Was it you who freed me?"

"Yes, it was I. But I only just escaped the same fate."

Michael then went on to relate how he managed to get the better of the old hag Jaga.

"Did you know, brother, that I am married?" asked Ivan.

"I certainly do!" Michael said laughingly. "I stopped at your palace. They all thought it was you who arrived, even your own wife, beautiful Marja. In fact she wanted me to kiss her! I did not disillusion her."

Ivan was very angry with his brother when he heard such words, "You are a bad brother! I don't wish to know you!"

He took his sword and severed Michael's head. Then he mounted his horse and rode home.

"Welcome back, Ivan," Marja cried. "How comes that you rode through here this morning, without uttering a single word, and crying bitterly? I hope you are now in a better mood."

Ivan Waters stopped abruptly, realizing that his brother certainly did not try to take his place. On the contrary, he was so choked with tears he could not even speak. All he could think of was to save his life. Ivan Waters swiftly turned his horse and rode like the wind back to the spot where he had severed his brother's head in unjust anger.

Vultures were already circling above Michael's body. Ivan jumped off his horse, caught one of the vultures' young, and cut off its head. Then he waited to see what would happen. An old vulture flew closer, croaked sadly to see the dead bird, then flew away. A moment later it returned, holding a rare herb in its beak. As soon as it touched the dead body of the baby bird, it was brought back to life and flew off happily. Ivan leapt upon the old vulture, took the herb from its beak and touched his brother with it. And Michael Waters was alive and well as before.

So the signs on the cross-roads were correct after all. Riches were waiting at the end of the first path, and death met them at the end of the other. What a lucky escape they both had!

Because it all ended so happily, a great feast was prepared. There was food in plenty and barrels twenty. They dined and wined for a week and a day, and laughed and danced the nights away.